Exile

ÇİLER İLHAN

EXILE

Translated from the Turkish by
Ayşegül Toroser Ateş

istrosbooks

English language edition first published by
Istros Books
London, United Kingdom www.istrosbooks.com

Originally published in Turkish as *Sürgün*, 2010

© Çiler İlhan, 2015

The right of Çiler İlhan to be identified as the author of this work has been
asserted in accordance with the Copyright, Designs and Patents Act, 1988

Translation © Ayşegül Toroser Ateş

Edited by Feyza Howell and S.D. Curtis

Cover design: Davor Pukljak, www.frontispis.hr

ISBN: 978-1-908236-25-8 (print edition)
ISBN: 978-1-908236-89-0 (eBook)

**This project has been funded with support from the TEDA Programme of
the Ministry of Culture and Tourism of the Republic of Turkey.**

Supported using public funding by
**ARTS COUNCIL
ENGLAND**

LOTTERY FUNDED

Contents

For those exiled from their homes, their homelands, their bodies, and their souls...
in the hope that they may return to their homelands within.

EXILE

'Exile is the unhealable rift forced between a human being and its native place, between the self and its true home: its essential sadness can never be surmounted.'

Edward Said[*]

* Said, Edward. 'The Mind of Winter,' Harper's Magazine, September 1984.

Zobar and Başa

It's been so long since the drums and pipes fell silent in Hatice Sultan. Yesterday my Zobar and me, we went to take a look at our old neighbourhood. There's no one left. Even Uncle Aziz has moved to Taşoluk... Zeynep, Gülfidan, Ertan Abi, every last one...

Aunt Emine had been the first one to leave. She moved to Izmir, to live with her daughter. Hers was the first house to be demolished. Then it was the turn of Gülbahar. Turned out onto the street in the middle of winter with two children, her house pulled down in the early hours, regardless of her tears.

Mustafa Abi turned out to be stubborn. He's still in Neslişah with his wife and daughter, but the old coffee house's closed down. Had he not owned his house he'd have been cooped up in Taşoluk a long time ago, like so many tenants. No one knows how long he'll hold out. Some bloke or other comes over every day, asking him to sell his house.

Mother Milay and Coro moved to Edirne. When Mother Milay insisted she'd never live in Taşoluk, they took Yilo, Lola and the grave of Dobru and moved early one mornin'. I cried buckets over them. After all, we'd come to know them as our mother and father ever since I was five and Zobar seven. They'd taken care of us ever since they snatched us out of the clutch of the Grim Reaper back in Romania, so how could I not cry? My sweet Tinke kept licking my tears as I cried... 'Come with us, we won't move if you don't come with us,' they said; especially Mother Milay who insisted we go, pleading for days – 'don't make me leave my heart back here' – but we didn't want to. We liked Istanbul; 'besides, we've grown up, we can look after ourselves,' we said.

Soon, my Zobar, Cingo, Tinke and me, the whole gang, we're gonna collect paper. In Taksim. We've been going up to Taksim ever since we moved to Dolapdere. But because I had a miscarriage, I can't walk far. That's how things are for now: It occurred to me afterwards that Mother Milay knew I was pregnant when we

9

got married, 'Are you pregnant or what, girl?' she'd asked, but I'd paid no attention: She doesn't miss a trick, does she?

Thank God the weather is fine. Cingo's not fussed but Tinke's over the moon. Her tail goes pat, pat, pat non-stop now she's seen the sun.

My Zobar's been so absent-minded ever since we moved here. He doesn't talk much, but he's been eating his heart out, I know. He dug his heels in so we wouldn't leave the neighbourhood, you know – 'we'll find a way to stay,' he'd said to me, so he's tried everything he could lately just so he could keep his word. You crazy boy, did you really think I'd keep my hopes up just because you said so? How were we to stay when the landlord had already sold our house? All the neighbourhood had taken off; how could we have stayed? Don't I miss my house in Hatice Sultan too? Don't I just? In fact, from time to time, I can't help but cry. That's when my Zobar takes me into his huge arms and says, 'Don't cry my beautiful Başa, we'll go back to our Sulukule some day, we will for sure, you'll see.' But I know: Sulukule now belongs to others.

This morning, I realized that crying's no help either. I whispered in my Zobar's ear 'Come, almond eyes, let *ourselves* be our homeland.'

CRIME

Iraq II

By the time the Americans came to Iraq, I'd long given up hope for both Iraq and for that scum who called himself a 'father'. I was pleased. Pleased that piece of filth might finally get his just desserts. My sister Rana and I never got over the pain of losing our husbands.

Stupid me! Just goes to show I still hadn't learnt my lesson after having seen so much wickedness even from my closest. Just goes to show I'd failed to understand how power makes the sons of Adam lose their humanity, turns them into demons. Just goes to show I'd failed even to imagine how ruthless foreigners would some day give birth to the demons within, how they would take to the streets and feast endlessly on these lands, these holy lands where civilisations once took root. It just goes to show that I didn't realize that the soldiers who would go for their bullets, making no exception for children, and who would go for their zips, with no respect for mothers or daughters, would cast their humanity off and become possessed. It just goes to show that I failed to envisage that my Iraq would from then on live by night, by night alone, as if now located at the poles, where the sun would never again be able to extend its fragile visage over daybreak.

And that boy from Karbala, whose big brother was taken away in a night raid; I dream of him every night; his pupils dilated, behind his mother with his kid brother, leaning against the wall. As if the wall would help him. He is shivering like a leaf in his pyjamas, but the screams are the mother's, crying for her elder son, who was taken from his house in the middle of the night to be carried first to torture and then to his death; what falls to his share is the silence of a grave. That dark-eyed boy in the newspaper who harbours in his eyes the sorrow of the world, the anxiety of the world. His picture won't leave my desk; nor his face my dreams. Oh my mighty Mesopotamia! Oh how they have hurt you.

Ball

We were playing ball. There was our Sülo, there was Mehmet, there was Fedai, there was Ramazan, and there was Raşit. There was my big brother and Raşit's big brother. That's where we always play ball. Sülo's team was winning again; doesn't he just love himself as he sneaks past! At that moment, I saw my brother and Raşit's brother wink at each other. I turned my head and looked; the gendarmes. I didn't pay any attention. They always come and take our ball when we're playing. We're used to it now. They'd taken my big brother and Raşit's to the station a couple of times and had beaten the living daylight out of them. They were forever accusing them of aiding the rebels, but they never do. Dad always kept us out of these conflicts. He'd promised mum before she died.

I thought the soldiers were going to take our ball again. But suddenly they started shooting. I saw my big brother on the ground. Five soldiers had surrounded him and were firing around his body. My brother had wrapped his arms tightly around his head. I tried to stop the soldiers. One of them punched me in the face and felled me. My brother tried to get up but they pushed him down. Then they started kicking him. Then they dragged him off into the minibus. They kept kicking him as they dragged him. I saw Mehmet running towards the village and I yelled after him, 'tell my father, tell him to get to the station immediately'. I started to run. The minibus speeded up. I ran all the way to the station. It's not far from where we play ball. They didn't let me in. I waited – then Dad came. They didn't let him in either. Ten minutes later the gendarme came over. Your son's heart has failed, must have had a heart condition, he told Dad. It's a lie. My brother was fit as a fiddle.

I'm a Bastard!

I'm a bastard! Literally a bastard! God, did I have to see my picture in the paper to realize this? The picture where I'm gagging that young girl? Newspapers said she was eighteen or twenty but she wasn't even seventeen! After she saw the photograph in the newspaper my wife rang the station and yelled at me, 'You're a bastard!' She said she was ashamed of me. I'm ashamed of myself too.

I just didn't think. My Boss had given us all strict instructions, 'Be on your guard during the Tunceli trip of Our Esteemed Minister, or I'll have you all!... Grab anyone that speaks, that squeaks, that stirs, that budges, or does anything at all and drag'em away!' he said. Then, when that girl suddenly cried 'Our Esteemed Minister!' while Our Esteemed Minister was speaking – and it was just my bleeding luck, I was right next to her, wasn't I – and I never thought, just shoved both hands over her mouth. And not just her mouth, either, I saw later in that photograph in the newspapers: I'd smothered her – her nose, her eyes – and she wore glasses too, and I grabbed them off in a rage! My mouth pursed in rage as if I'd kill her. And bugger it if our Inspector hadn't also heard her shouting 'Our Esteemed Minister!' and turned up right beside me ordering 'run her in straight away!' Chuffed to bits I was doing a great job, I was in his good books, you know, I dragged her away and stuffed her into the patrol car. Mind you, I was still proud of myself. Who could say she wasn't a separatist?

She started crying inside the car. I didn't give a damn. I was saying to myself, this little bitch will give us a couple of names now, who knows, we might even corner those responsible for yesterday's attack. How that would please my Boss! I'll boast about it to my wife.

We slammed her into a cell at once. Naturally, I joined the interview too; well, we caught her, we'll make her talk. She's in custody at the most infamous station, I was saying to myself, she has no choice but to spill the beans. And I'll become the pride of the station. Boy, was I proud of myself. An hour, two, three – not a word. She was crying buckets. 'I'm not a separatist or anything, all I wanted was to say to Our Esteemed Minister, "my family is not letting me go to university, please help me."' 'Look here,' I said firstly, 'pull the other one, you little bitch, it's got bells on.' So Ahmet and me, we tried all the tricks we knew: Anything, you name it but still, nothing.

Then someone pulled strings and we had to let her go after six hours. Without getting a word out of her. Yet at home I was still telling myself that there was definitely something fishy about this girl.

Dear God! Never realized how innocent her little face was! I never realized until I saw it in the newspaper.

You Killed

You killed my mother. You killed my father: My uncles and my aunts. You killed my grandmother and my grandfather: My cousins, their wives: My father's sisters, their husbands. You killed me within.

You killed my beloved, my husband, my love. You killed love.

You killed the flower within me.

You dried up the rain. You drained the water. I'm dried up.

You rooted out the tree of life our orphaned arms had nourished within us.

You cut the climbers we'd raised under each other's light, each other's shadow.

You destroyed the road along which we could never have walked without being united.

My days, my nights.

You imprisoned my breath.

You sewed my lips together.

My nails no longer grow.

You froze the lakes. You froze my blood.

My joy, my hope.

You froze me within.

You sucked out my soul.

You stole my old age.

My cheeks.

My cheeks hurt.

What has my Hrant* done to you?

You killed. You killed me too.

---

* Hrank Dink, a Turkish-Armenian journalist assassinated on 19 January 2007

Batman

'Why do so many women commit suicide in Batman?' they ask. There is nothing we can add to life, other than death.

We are invisible at home and in the street. Like an old piece of rag that cleans the floors, the windows, the doors. We are put to all sorts of work. Life becomes even more unbearable once we start to blossom, once we are fragrant. Bored with our mothers, whose breasts have sagged, whose flesh has lost their firmness from giving birth a dozen times, the gazes of our fathers alight on our newly budding breasts. Suddenly our mothers go blind, our brothers deaf.

'Why do so many women commit suicide in Batman?' they ask. There is nothing you can add to our life, other than death.

When we grow a little older we are married into other families. But we are found not to be virgins, for we are not. And in the morning of that very same night, we are dumped back in front of our fathers' doors like milk that has gone sour. What a calamity! The dirty linen could not be kept secret, the true colours are revealed; the world is set ablaze. A scapegoat from among the destitute, the poorest wretch in the village is used to restore the family honour; this dog deflowered my lovely daughter on this and this date, before she could give herself to her husband, he is to be blamed! Yet words don't suffice to clear the honour of a family. Someone must be hurt, blood must be shed. So that all should believe that the house the girl came from is immaculate.

The family elders speak: The boy who deflowered our girl on this and this date has a sister – doesn't matter that she's eleven or twelve, she's a woman – we will deflower her.

One morning, as she's out fetching water from the well, the wretch's sister is held down and raped, with the help of the female relatives if necessary (what is there to be surprised at, after a point there's no telling what's right and what's wrong) – so that everything fits into place. So that the father of the deflowered girl can brag: Mehmet, we know your son deflowered my daughter on this and this date, my honour has been avenged, we have deflowered your girl in return. We're even.

'Why do so many women commit suicide in Batman?' they ask. Instead, you should ask: Is a man's blood sweeter than that of a woman?

Then an agreement is made to avoid a vendetta, so that guns are not fired in our peaceful, exemplary villages, so that the dear blood of the men would not spill from their precious veins on to the earth, so that no disgrace is brought upon the clan, with court appearances and newspaper coverage and all, so that they wouldn't have to deal with the gendarmes or the journalists: the sister of such and such a youth married her rapist who raped her near the fountain, and the maid-no-more is given to the poor wretch who allegedly raped her on this and this date.

'Why do so many women commit suicide in Batman?' they ask.

My Daughter

When I looked for my daughter one morning, I realized she was not around. I thought to myself, where's she bleeding gone again, at the crack of dawn? She was always out, and never listened to me. I went into her brothers' room; all three were sound asleep. I woke the eldest up, telling him he was late for work. I was surprised; he'd gone to bed with his clothes on, just like that, just as he'd come home from work. 'Do you know where your sister is?' I asked. He just stared. 'Mother, come, there's something we have to tell you,' he said. He woke up his brothers too. 'Go and pour us some tea,' he said. I was scared of the way he sounded. I went into the kitchen and poured some tea for the three of them.

'Mother, we killed our sister, there was no other way out, she was bringing shame upon our family,' he said.

Suddenly my blood pressure rose, I felt I was about to collapse. They gathered around me, rubbed my hands and arms with cologne. When I came round, I started repeating: 'Oh God, please let it be a dream, let me wake up... Oh God, God forbid.'

Repeating *bismillah* over and over again, I ran into my daughter's room. She wasn't there. I went back to the kitchen. Her three brothers were staring intently at my face. The youngest started sobbing.

'Mother, you keep our secret,' said the eldest.

I sat there and cried my eyes out, oh God, what else was I going to do. But there is no escape from fate. In the end I decided, what could I do, I'm a mother and I've lost my daughter, let me at least not lose my other children. And so I have not said a word to anyone for nine years. I'm so very sorry.

Baby Girl

Some kind-heart had brought us a whole load of leftovers and we were full. In good spirits, I mean. Us stray dogs can't always find something to eat. Some days we just cannot, you understand, but that day we had; lucky us. And as we had nothing else to do, we were chillin'.

We found ourselves in the cemetery. Suddenly Abhi, he's the one with the strongest sense of smell among us (now, I *am* the leader, but give credit where it's due), started barking for no apparent reason. He never barks for nothing. On my command, my pack trotted over to where he was. The smell of the living! Impossible! Now, we are able to distinguish the smell of the newly buried from that of a person buried two days ago, that of a five-days buried from that of a one-month buried, five years from ten years; we're good like that, you see. But this smell coming from under the earth was clearly that of the living!

Immediately, on my command, my pack started digging with all four paws. Imagine, eight dogs, all barking and digging the earth in unison. Thank God we managed to attract the attention of some passer-by; otherwise, the smell of the living was coming from deep below and who knows how much longer we'd have tried. There's no telling if the human being would still have been alive by then. That man who saw us from a distance and suspected something fishy came near us. Thankfully he got suspicious at our anxiety and attitude. He ran out of the cemetery and came back with the police. A swarm of policemen, picks and shovels in their hands, they wanted us to stand aside: On my command, my pack all stepped aside. In a flash, they dug the earth we'd been pawing.

And what d'you think they found? A tiny human puppy! How happy we were. The police chief tagged me as the leader, and gave me enough bones to feed my pack. That was some lucky day.

Number 5

I am Han. I must admit it's an ironic name, King, for someone whose life was threatened even in his mother's womb.

Here is what happened: apparently my mother and father were members of the Gene Purging Programme, under which, my gene tests were carried out as soon as it was understood that I had been conceived. The device did not give out a signal. Everyone was happy: 'Your fifth seed is pure, there, you may give birth.' But I fooled you there, didn't I!

The pregnancy was uneventful; I made sure of that. I didn't make the slightest noise in there so that I wouldn't cause any suspicion. I gave my mother neither morning sickness nor a single sleepless hour: In fact, I didn't even grow to my full extent, so that she would remain totally comfortable. Oh, how happy my mother was, how happy everyone was. Well, after all it was a pure gene, and these pure genes are really something. Good thing we joined this programme. Look at Ayşe, poor woman, how plagued by flatulence she is.

I waited. To tell you the truth, I waited quite a long time. I believed that if I waited for nine months I would be sure to get out no matter what. After all, by then I would officially be considered a human being! By the end of the ninth month my hands were slightly overgrown, and I was tired of making them into fists so that my mother's belly would not swell too much; so I loosened them a little bit. Not entirely, mind you, just a little bit, just to get a little more comfortable. How I wish I hadn't! My mother, who'd been having a really easy time of it, like a princess, suddenly rushed off to the doctor at this sudden discomfort in her belly, ordering my father to 'Come quickly!' over the phone. Those white-shirts, they love pontificating on such matters, they can't get enough of it; so they got together at once. That a baby with purged genes should cause discomfort! Impossible! The white-shirts became suspicious. 'No', they said, 'no, there is something wrong here'. That famous device was brought in straight away, the belly was listened to, glances were exchanged secretly and words were exchanged openly. There has been a terrible mistake! A one-in-a-million kind of thing. You must have understood by the fact that the device gave out a signal; your baby's genes are not pure!

My mother was furious, with that huge belly of hers! 'How could such a thing happen? A bagful of money was spent on this programme!'

'We are very sorry, madam, you will get a refund immediately.'

They went on coaxing her for hours to no avail; my mother would have none of it. While she was storming at the doctors I suddenly realized that my father had already slipped away. That's what he does, my father gets lost whenever things get messy, I have observed it over these past nine months. When my mother finally noticed his absence she jumped into her car in a panic, naturally she did not listen to the doctors' orders about not driving. She started driving and calling my father on her mobile, but there was no answer. Now she cannot stand that, she cannot stand my father ignoring her; but it's not because she adores her husband, it's because she has to keep up appearances. 'Sweetie,' she often tells her friends, 'I can't remember a single night when we didn't sleep cuddling, hand in hand. In all these years we've not had a serious argument or disagreement.' There is bound to be no disagreement if you keep being such a witch!

But this time she's in deep trouble; the baby is flawed, the husband is gone, she's been disgraced before her colleagues. She is actually quite delicate, and it must have been her hormones or something (after all she is pregnant) for even I couldn't have predicted it, and my baby's instincts are very powerful. In the blink of an eye she veered the car towards a cliff! I still do not know whether she was angrier with me or with herself.

But her plan didn't work, I didn't die! I didn't! By the time the air ambulance arrived my mother had already breathed her last. The blue shirts immediately opened up her belly there and then and took out what was inside. Me – blind, but full of life.

The Seed

Into whose soul it was first cast I know not. Yet what I know suffices for me. All the same, I will not bore you by telling you everything I know.

Although not altogether certain, it is possible that it all started with my father's father's father's father. And that is because I can only retrace our genealogy back to him. My conviction is that it goes even further back. The mountains, however, conceal footprints well, that is true, but my father's father's father's father was a nomad.

Legend has it that the budding of the seed of evil began with my grandfather Nusrahit when he murdered his wife. Quite out of the blue he slit her throat one night while she was asleep. Was he already sick but didn't show it? Or had the sickness taken hold of him in a single day as if he was possessed by a demon? No one knows. What *is* known is that he woke up (whatever got into him) from his sleep (whatever he might have been dreaming of) and sunk the knife he used to cut sheep and goats with into Mother Haşimet's throat. It's the mountains. There's no gendarme, no police. What were they to do? He must be punished for the sake of peace among the nomads. Kabil, the elder son, took on the job of punishment, but there was to be no killing, no rape, and no torture. What else is there? Crude beating. Kabil beat his father to death. Yet, there is something strange here; Nusruhat, the younger son, told the Elders that one night he had seen Kabil and his mother embracing, that his father was most probably aware of this sin and that's why he killed Mother Haşimet. But then, the daughter of the house took the floor. She claimed that Kabil and her mother could not have been lovers because Kabil was in love with her. And Kabil (perhaps to save his neck) admitted that he belonged to Zenina. And when the Elders asked him to prove his love he gave his sister a long kiss on the lips.

It appears Kabil's hands had not been wetted enough with his own father's blood, word goes round that he also sold Temcit, his daughter born of his wife (not of Zenina, for he did not marry her) to the bandits in exchange for ten goats. We do not know where the bandits took the girl. The greatest evil, however, lies not in giving Temcit to the bandits but in stripping her of her tongue as well. Because Temcit always contradicted her father, because she never paid him filial respect, because she always humiliated him publicly and told everyone how *he* beat *his* father, grandfather Nusrahit to death, Kabil was full of resentment towards this ungrateful girl. On the night before the morning he would deliver her to the bandits he put her to sleep (who knows with what) and cut her tongue off with the knife he slaughtered sheep and goats with. And to make sure she would not bleed to death before she was delivered to her new owner, he wrapped the wound up thoroughly. Temcit woke up the next morning to find that she had no tongue. The bandits took her away as she was, no tongue and all.

Damdız, was the younger one of the two sons Surtun, and Damdız, the quiet one, the kind-hearted, the skilful, the one who looked after the family – the kind to watch out for.

Damdız was not troubled with his wife like his grandfather Nusrahit or with his daughter like his father Kabil. They say he is a pederast. Rumour has it that this story is true. As Damdız is very handsome, all the girls in the tribe are crazy for him. But he only had eyes for one: Kunduz. Kunduz was married though. He had a gorgeous wife with hair down to her waist, long legs and sky-blue eyes. And Kunduz only had eyes for her. One day, mustering up all his courage, Damdız told Kunduz about the fire that was burning him up.

But what did Kunduz do? He rained all kinds of insults at him. He must have given him a couple of blows too, I believe, for Kunduz was that kind of man. Then, not having been able to vent his spleen, he went and told everyone that Damdız was a pederast. Damdız was devastated, not because all the tribe found out that he was a pederast, but because he had been so badly slighted by the object of his affections. One day, as Kunduz's beauteous wife Aybalam was grazing the goats, he took the woman forcibly (even though he could hardly find it in him). But that's not where the greatest evil lies: he did this when Kunduz was around, so that he would come too. Then, taking out the knife he used to slaughter sheep and goats with, he cut Kunduz's statuesque manhood at its root. It is said that Kunduz bled to death and that his wife threw herself off a cliff of shame and a broken heart, after giving birth to the baby inside her.

This child of rape, Sülyon (for whatever reason the tribe named him so), happens to be my father. If you ask me whether that seed of evil has passed down to him, I do not know for certain, but the fondness for cutting certainly has! For if it had not been for that, why else when waking up one night (who knows whatever got into him), would he have violated me at the point of the knife he used to cut the strings of the mushroom sacks!

Dimwits

I told these buggers, 'if you must do it, do it on the quiet', I said. But do they have that sort of sense? If they did, they wouldn't be giving inadequate sermons in ruined parish churches for years – they'd be the Pope, like me. I had to pontificate so much to hush it all up: about Iraq, about the civil war in Sudan, about the seminary in Turkey, about Muslim terrorists. But it seems a bunch of journalists have it in for me. Faggots. So what if my men have groped a couple of children? Doesn't this ever happen in Islamic orders? They say I've sheltered paedophiliac clerics! They say I hushed up criminal records during my tenure as a cardinal with the admonition: 'Always keep under lock and key. Top secret.' They grope their pupils at schools, their patients in their clinics, and their own children in their homes to their hearts' content, and then clamour at me to clear their consciences. Everyone envies the Vatican. They envy our power just as they envy our gold-embroidered clothes and our spectacular sceptre.

Wreck

I told mum. 'This boat is not safe, it won't take us there and back,' I said. 'Let's not board it,' I said. 'I have a bad feeling about it!'. 'You think you know better than your father? He says it's safe,' she said. 'Now stop complaining and help me get these pies on board,' she said. 'Buzzing like a hornet around my head again,' she said. My big brother made fun of me, saying, 'well, she a girl isn't she, scaredy-cat'. My kid brother – he's the only one who opened his eyes and looked at me.

All of a sudden the weather turned. A storm broke out of nowhere; how and where, we never understood. Mum can't swim. My big brother jumped after his father who fell overboard. They didn't surface. But I felt a strength from within, I swam, and swam, and swam.

My big sister – she'd dug her heels in, refusing to get on the boat with us. She hates the sea. She'd run away and hidden again, risking a beating by dad on our return. She called the coastguard when the storm broke. They pulled me aboard, not far from the shore, just as the strength in my arms failed.

Mum, dad, my big brother... it's not them... but I feel like cutting off that hand of mine which slipped out of my fourteen-year-old brother's grip.

Pippa

It was me. I killed Pippa. By disclaiming her as soon as she was conceived. By moving heaven and earth to stop her from being born; existing after she is born.

I noticed her too late anyway. I had let her grow inside me for four months unawares. I begged the doctor: get this thing out of me, I pleaded, but he wouldn't. In our Catholic village there were only a few doctors who would do the job anyway. And my doctor said: 'this has grown too much, I can't abort it now.'

I didn't give up. I did everything I knew, everything I had heard of. We all did. My mother helped. Hot water, kicking, whatever we could think of but nothing worked. It was impudent, it was shameless. It just wouldn't be miscarried.

It grew and grew within me, like a demon, like a monster. I hated it. I hated it before it was even born. My life was already difficult; it was difficult enough without it. I had gone back to live with my parents when my husband threw me out. In actual fact, my mother wanted neither me nor my four daughters. My father was tenderer at heart and it was thanks to him that we were allowed to stay. But had she known I had gone to her house expecting again, my mother wouldn't have let me in in the first place.

Finally, months later, I was rent open and Pippa came out. With great ease, as if she knew she wasn't safe inside me and wanted to throw herself out as soon as possible, she just popped out. She was such a small baby, so feeble; a lump of flesh, something ugly. I went dry the first week. After her four big sisters I had neither the breast to give her nor the will to give it.

It was because of her that I quit my job at Banca di Roma. It was a busy branch and my director appreciated me. And it was because of her that my mother and I fell out again. When I stopped bringing home money, my mother wanted us even less.

I didn't want to go back to my husband. I had no place to go other than the house of my mother who didn't want me. I did not want this baby.

When she was thirty-two days old, towards the evening one day, I pressed a pillow against her face. My mother thought of it. It would look as if she smothered herself burying her face in the pillow in her sleep, 'come, let's do that,' she said. Or was it me who said that? I don't remember. I pressed the pillow against her face. She was so tiny anyway. She just had a teeny-weeny bit of life in her. Just as we were thinking that she'd be gone in less than a minute, can you believe it, my aunt came in! She pounced upon me like an eagle! She threw the pillow aside and slapped me. She swore at my mother. My mother swore at her: 'Why do you interfere, are you going to look after it?' While they were fighting the baby suddenly made a sound. That baby that hadn't made a sound for thirty-two days, not even when she was born, and this time she made a strange sound. It was neither a cry nor a laugh. Just a plain sound. I froze within. It was at that moment that I realized that I wouldn't be able to get rid of this child.

When my mother sent me back to my husband's house immediately after my father died, her father gave Pippa the cold shoulder too. But her eldest sister always kept her by her side; buggered if I knew what she found to like about her. She grew up like Thumbelina, just like that. Neither in her childhood nor in her youth was she beautiful, and she became the laughing stock of her friends when her face was covered with pimples at the age of twelve. But her big sister still didn't let anyone speak ill of her. She kept on reading books, going to exhibitions; she had her head in the clouds all the time. Why doesn't she do something useful instead of reading books all the time, I asked her sister a few times, but then realizing there was no hope I let her stew in her own juice, what do I care?

What I mean to say is, frankly, I wasn't really surprised. She was an artist, supposedly. Two friends, they were planning to sew themselves wedding dresses and give out peace messages while hitchhiking. Her sister tried hard to persuade her that it was dangerous, but to no avail. She had set her mind on it.

They called on the telephone. We were about to sit down for supper with her father. Her big sister and her fiancée found out from the friend with whom she had set out on her journey that she was in Turkey last and had called the police. Apparently, she had been missing for twelve days. The Turkish police found her. Somewhere near Istanbul a lorry driver who had given her a lift had raped her and then strangled her. He dumped her in the forest.

A day before she set out on her journey she had phoned me and said, 'if anything happens to me let my four sisters carry my coffin'. Hogging the limelight even as she departs.

The Undying

She just won't die, the bitch! She neither dies nor does she give in. I just broke her fingers, but to no effect. What spirit the bitch has. I'd have thrown in the sponge a thousand times by now.

She was just a small girl when she first came to the shop. How beautiful she was, the coquette. She couldn't have been more than fifteen. Her buttocks and all had taken shape, so round. Quite coy, too. It was still her first week; how could one resist her. 'You stole money,' I said. 'I'll hand you in to the police if you don't do as I say,' I said. 'They'll separate you from your mother, put you in a reformatory. Do you know how they beat children up there? Didn't you see it on the news, how they scalded the children with hot water,' I said. 'The things they would do to you! They hate pretty girls there,' I said. She was scared stiff. 'Right,' I said, and I went for it. Nothing like the taste of a virgin.

She's been with me for five years now. As she grew older, she stopped falling for the reformatory lie, of course. Then, I said, 'I'll tell your mother. I'll say your whore of a daughter seduced me,' said I. 'I'll say she has quite a reputation in Beyoğlu anyway.' She shakes in her boots in front of her mother. So I managed to fool her this way for another couple of years. Still, we wouldn't have been on bad terms... If it wasn't for one of the tradesmen...

'What's it got to do with you, you bastard! Why don't you mind your own business!'

'No, come, and we'll talk it out. We might come to an agreement, right?'

'You beast!'

One day, he came to the shop while we were at the back. Apparently, he became suspicious when I rushed out in a sweat. And what should I see the next day; he was pacing up and down in front of my shop. He hung around for a few more days, seeing her at the counter he must have caught on; 'almost the same age as my girl'. To cut a long story short, the bastard threatened me. 'I'll hand you in to the police, I'll take you to court,' he said. 'I talked to the girl, she didn't consent,' he said. Whenever did those two get the chance to talk? Wait, man, I thought to myself, now let's not get wrapped up in this too. Let's not bring trouble upon ourselves. Let me just marry the little doodad.

But despite all that... No, no, no! What bloody-mindedness! I said this, I said that; nothing worked! I swear, I bought her gold coins, bracelets... No, no, no!

'What's wrong with marrying, man? Have you known any other man but me? Besides, penetrated as you are, who else is going to marry you around here anyway? Well, it's not that I'm not handsome, to be fair... just marry me!'

'No, I won't, no, I won't.'

I told her mother. 'Look,' I said, 'it is so and so. Your daughter seduced me and, you know, things happened... well, at this stage you can't marry her off to anyone else. Let me marry her – a clean job. I'll look after you too... we'll both be satisfied.'

'I'd already realized it,' she said.

'Piss off! If you had, would you have kept quiet until now? You'd have blackmailed bagfuls of money out of me by now!'

Anyway, I slipped a hundred bucks into her hand. 'Your daughter will be staying with me for a while, you divert the people in the neighbourhood telling them she's gone to your village and so on,' I said. 'Come and see her when you feel like it,' I added.

I grappled for exactly two months. Turned into a battle of wills too. I grew tired of her obstinacy. And as I grew tired I started to hurt her even more. During the day I tied her to the bed so she couldn't run away. During the night I worked myself to the bone. Stubbed out cigarettes on her skin – still she said no. Beat her half dead – no. Slashed her here and there with a razorblade – no.

My younger daughter who is tenderhearted, rarely comes over to my place; however, one day, I think she needed something, and she decided to come over... what will be will be. They both have the key to my apartment although they don't really visit often. At least they can get in without breaking the door open if I should die or something. Anyway, my younger daughter came and saw her, of course. The girl was all tears, pleading. My daughter cut her hair off; so I grabbed her instead by the hair and smashed her against the wall, didn't I? Women – birdbrains the lot of them. Shit, wouldn't I find somewhere else to hold her by if she didn't have her hair! Is her hair all I've got, for goodness' sake?

Exhausted

No one can be as exhausted as I am. When did I get so exhausted?

The weight of the money I have stolen weighs down on my chest. The faces I've knocked about. The arms that didn't want to let go of the handles of their cheap leather bags, the arms I had to dislocate.

The heartbeats of the people I followed step by step in deserted alleys deafen me. Eyes that popped out as if they'd seen a ghost. My lips are chewed every night by the lips that trembled in despair, while snot and tears flowed rapidly down their chins. The non-existent hair of the bald men whose skulls I cracked the moment they came across me in the corridors of their own houses at the most unexpected moment gets between my teeth. Those young, tender girls sleeping with their waists exposed in their very thin nightdresses, they are prepared to surrender anything but themselves, anything to stop that poison-stinking hand shutting their mouths, touching their flesh. Whenever I go to the toilet a sour taste comes to my mouth at the memory of the urine released by the children who were sleeping in their blue–pink rooms, cuddling their teddy-bears when they saw my shadow near the dim night lamps turned on by their mothers so that they wouldn't be afraid in the dark.

It always surprises me how the old people who start queuing at six in the morning just to be able to to draw their pensions five hours later, whose feet barely carry their bones, each hang on to their mouthful of breath when I grab them tightly by the wrist as they try to walk to the cheap public busses that would take them home. The flesh I feel under my touch is close to disintegrating; my flesh disintegrates bit by bit with each new touch. Each morsel I prevent them from eating sticks in my throat. Each tarmac scratch on the delicate skins of the women I drag along the ground turns into a deep scar on my skin. Each insult suffered in Laleli by the Moldavian women who lost their jobs because of the money I stole from the villas of the rich, into which I sneak as quiet as a snake in the small hours of the morning, sticks on my face like snot. When I steal from his pocket the first salary some well-off youth has just drawn from the bank, I know that it's not his money that I've stolen; it's his faith. My own dream is depleted with each dream I steal. With each pride that is pierced with each bullet I fire into the leg of each hero wanting to defend the safe, the hole in my heart gets bigger.

I'm exhausted. The face of that child I killed by mistake does not stop haunting me.

Donation

Which one of you came up with the idea of making soldiers out of us? Asking for us from our owners, from our patriotic owners, as donations? 'We'll even pay for them if they turn out to be promising as soldiers', you said. And we thought they loved us as much as we loved them. Many of your good citizens whom you paralysed through fear gave us up after a single campaign.

We, the donations, were gathered in the Dog Training Centre of the Ministry of Defence. Some of us saw it straight away; this was no vacation. Some of our owners decided against giving their friends away as soldiers at the last moment. Mine didn't.

They made us play games, so to speak, and divided us into three categories. We realized that those who wouldn't let go of the ball under any circumstances would be trackers; the fastest would be used to catch runaways; and those who are absent-minded would be used in the dirtiest jobs by the Pentagon, the building in which we were housed. Pentagon, what a gracious host you are.

We were put under a strict programme. Little food, lots of training. Little food, lots of training. Little food, lots of training. This is what we are. You bipeds wouldn't understand. We love and miss our owners no matter what they do. We missed them. We also missed those concrete walls you call homes, no offence, and which we protected on pain of death. We missed our food that smells so good but is all hollowed out after so much processing, we missed our bones, our toys, our yellow balls, our soft beds. And the Pentagon's guesthouse turned out not to be as comfortable as our owners were promised it would be. They didn't even give us mattresses, whereas back home most of us would sleep in our parents' beds.

After four-months of training, we donations gradually started active duty. We awaited each return anxiously. The fact that no one in the first battalion that came back was harmed gave us a little comfort. The ones in the second battalion came back with slight wounds or missing limbs: one of them came back with the right hind leg severed, another with a dismembered ear. When it was our battalion's turn they took only one soldier for the first mission. Two days went by, it did not come back. On the third day they sent another soldier on a mission, it did not come back. A third, a fourth, a fifth – they did not come back.

I've been absent-minded all my life; is that a crime? All the other Retrievers were chosen for the tracker battalion. My mind, however, does not stay on track, it just wanders off; if it didn't, or if I were very agile, or if I could run fast enough to catch the bad guys, these bombs wouldn't have to be tied to my belly right now. The remote control, in the hands of my own trainer too. We spent four months together! Aren't you going to feel the least bit sad when my bones are scattered on the streets? Just so you can blame this unsolved case on some jihadist group or other, on suicide bombers blown to smithereens?

Sai Bo Gu Ji Man Gwen Chan A*

Herman the bull, **the first farm animal** to carry human genes was put to sleep due to an arthritis attack. One of his genes was replaced with a human gene while he was still an embryo. The objective was to make the milk of Herman's progeny contain human protein. Human protein was found in the milk of the progeny but it was understood that it was a *negligibly small amount*. American researchers constructed the gene map of a laboratory rat of the species *Rattus norvegicus*. Kerstin Lindblad, a **GENETIC ENGINEER** from the Whitehead Institute, in referring to the gene mapping of laboratory mice – the third mammal to be thus mapped after the humans and rats – said, 'this is of enormous significance in decoding human physiology and pathology.' The research on the production of animate beings containing computer chips (**Cyborg**), carried out at the Massachusetts Institute of Technology in the USA nears completion. *The spy moths* that grow with the microchips inserted into them while still in the cocoon will be remote controlled and guided as required. With the help of the spy moths thus produced it will be possible to hunt down terrorists in the mountains at the end of nowhere in the north of Pakistan, for instance. Scientists have enabled moths to grow with the microchips inserted into them while still in the cocoon. The Pentagon is pleased with the research. Rod Brooks, head of the MIT Computer Sciences and Artificial Intelligence Laboratory said: 'Animate robot research is cheaper than producing nuclear weapons. Moths eat very little and can fly everywhere. We had carried out similar research on rats and cockroaches in the past but the growth and development of a butterfly with the chip inside it has been achieved for the first time.' **Top 3 in design**: Labradoodle, Puggle, Maltapoo. These dogs that are bred through the cross-mating of the Labrador and the standard Poodle can command

---

* Original title of the 2006 film *'I'm a Cyborg, But That's OK'* by Park Chan-Wook

a price of up to 2500 dollars. The Labrador's qualities of conformity as a guide dog have been brought together with the Poodle's *antiallergenic coat* that does not moult. This species was bred for the first time in Australia 30 years ago. The cross-breed of the Beagle and the Pug, the most popular design dog, is the Puggle. Due to its small body it *is the perfect dog for those who live in flats*. It was created by decreasing the Pug's bulging eyes and combining the Beagle's instinct of running and moving. Maltapoo, on the other hand, is Jessica Simpson's choice. These dogs incorporate the responsible character of the Poodle and the playful nature and gentle character of the Maltese. Nevertheless, not all dogs are designer dogs; **beware of fake designs**. For a dog to be called 'designer,' it must be created through the cross-breeding of the genetically healthiest and strongest, and of course the most amiable members of two different pure breeds. The genes that carry genetic diseases or undesirable character streaks are eliminated before mating. By combining the best ones, one **PERFECT DOG** is created. The dogs that were starved for days at the Kuşadası Municipality Dog Shelter tore each other to pieces. The private company that had undertaken the feeding of the 240 dogs in the dog shelter stopped delivering when their contract ended on December 31. Seven dogs were torn to pieces when the dogs that spent the holiday hungry and without keepers attacked each other. Thirty dogs, on the other hand, are still missing. Herman the bull, the first farm animal to carry human genes was put to sleep due to an arthritis attack. One of his genes was replaced with a human gene while he was still an embryo. The objective was to make the milk of Herman's progeny contain human protein. Human protein was found in the milk of the progeny but it was understood that it was a *negligibly small amount*. American researchers constructed the gene map of a laboratory rat of the species *Rattus norvegicus*. Kerstin Lindblad, a **GENETIC ENGINEER** from the Whitehead Institute, in referring to the gene mapping of laboratory mice—the third mammal to be thus mapped after the humans and rats- said, 'This is of enormous significance in decoding human physiology and pathology.' The research on the production of animate beings containing computer chips (**Cyborg**), carried out at the Massachusetts Institute of Technology in the USA nears completion. *The spy moths* that grow with the microchips inserted into them while still in the cocoon will be remote controlled and guided as required. With the help of the spy moths thus produced it will be possible to hunt down terrorists in the mountains at the end of nowhere in the north of Pakistan, for instance. Scientists have enabled moths to grow with the microchips inserted into them while still in the cocoon. **The Pentagon** is **pleased** with the research. Rod Brooks, head of the MIT Computer Sciences and Artificial Intelligence Laboratory said: 'Animate robot research is cheaper than producing nuclear weapons. Moths eat very little and can fly everywhere.'

Sincerity

She went out through the main entrance at 08.15 as she did every weekday morning. It was a rainy day; a day on which rain, which fills even those who least like it with joy after a dry summer, is given the seat of honour in every house, like an important guest.

She walked towards the entrance to the parking lot. She stepped on to the pavement. She turned her head left and started waiting for a taxi. As usual, she came across a free taxi after only a few cars had passed by. So many taxis go by this street, it's incredible. If she wasn't still sleepy she would have noticed that the taxi driver was smoking while driving, before she waved at the taxi and would have pretended not to be waiting for a taxi; however, that morning she had got up late because she had gone to bed late. Not that she had had anything important to do; it was because she'd been trying to prove to herself that she was making enough time for herself after work. And because she went to bed late woke up late and didn't do any of the stuff that usually gets her ready for the day (having coffee, listening to strange *R&B* songs on *MCM Top*, doing a few stretching exercises) and got herself straight into the shower, then in front of the huge mirror in the living room and out the door, she did not wake up to the fact that the taxi driver was smoking, and in the meantime the taxi had stopped and she had got in. Again, if she had been a little bit more awake, she would have warned the taxi driver with a calm but firm tone of voice that if he was going to continue smoking she would get out of his taxi and get into another one, but the taxi happened to have moved on a few metres already before she could think of it.

She opened the window, but couldn't be bothered to chide herself for not paying attention. The taxi's wheels had rolled a few more times when she caught sight of a dog passing by on the pavement. The dog looked truly miserable. She'd soon find out from the vet: mites or blood worms – the dog was inundated with some pest, gnawed raw, even gnawed through the skin and the flesh was pierced. Who knows what else they'd done. Even though the dog could not be called skin and bones compared to any other stray dog, it was certainly skin and bones compared to her own dogs for instance, and it would stop and scratch itself every few steps. In fact, from the scene that she saw when she opened the window and looked back as the taxi moved on, she understood how long the life of this poor thing had been this way. She knew it from experience with her younger dog that had once been infested by mites; once the itching came the dog would not care for anything, even if the world's tastiest food was there in front of it; it would only want to scratch itself, scratch, scratch. She hesitated for a second, but she did not tell the taxi driver to stop. The taxi moved on, towards her workplace. Her stomach ached all through the day whenever she thought of the dog's erupted, open wounds and its face full of wounds. As happens to her when she is very upset, she was breathless. She stopped, tried to breathe, couldn't again, stopped, and tried to forget, as one does with many of the things we think will disappear if we don't see them.

Being a typical weekday, she was heading home in a taxi. Her mind was blank, and it was nearing seven o'clock. At the end of the seven-minute journey the taxi went into the parking lot. Pleased she would not be arguing with the driver over the change, she took the exact amount of cash out of her purse and gave it to him (she had not ever come across a single female driver in Istanbul). She said 'good evening' politely, but keeping her usual distance, and got out. She was as happy as she was every day that a day at work had again ended in a way that could be considered well, that she was back home, that her husband would soon be home, and that in two minutes she'd be reunited with the dogs she'd been missing all day long.

She walked to the main entrance, pushed open the unlocked outer door, and taking her key out of her bag she first opened the always-locked building door, then her own door. As usual, the younger dog jumped on her on two paws and the older one started shaking his bottom with joy, his cushion in his mouth. She pretended to be angry with both of them; this was part of the daily welcoming ritual. She was cross with one for jumping onto her, with the other for stealing the cushion. Then she fed them, knowing very well that they did not like it at all but because they could not go about in the Teşvikiye district's traffic any other way. She got their leashes over their heads with a sense of guilt, as if she was apologizing, patting them and kissing them, both tails wagging fit to drop off, joyfully as if they had eaten their first meal ever, as if it was the first time the world streets were to be roamed about, as if mother had not come round the house for years.

Then the three of them went out together. They peed in the back garden of the building straight away, took a walk towards the vet that was just a few streets away in an absurd state of pleasure. There was some jocular and some serious snarling on the way (because her young dog would bite anything she found), then her young dog, pooed on the pavement, unable to hold it until he found a bit of greenery as usual, and she picked up the poo with a plastic bag without touching it, then her older dog pooed but only after finding a bit of greenery, and again she picked up the big poo the same way. She relaxed when they had relaxed. They then went to the vet, where all three of them were received with a semi-sincere attention since they were regular customers. The dogs were paid the necessary compliments, the cyst pills, the flee and tick drops onto the neck were duly administered. At the cashier she had whatever she owed deducted from her credit card, she unwillingly held her dogs by their leashes again, and they went back home at a varying pace, sometimes with quick steps and at other times dawdling.

Her dogs, when they got home, wagged their tails rapidly, just as they did when they were going out. She was happy. She showed her happiness by saying, 'have we come home my babies,' with a soft, sweet tone of voice, which caused her dogs to wag their tails even more. In the mailbox she saw an envelope which she hadn't seen when she came home a short while before. I'll leave the dogs home and then I'll come out and get it, she thought. There was no one in the entrance, when she took the leashes off her dogs' necks not losing a moment. Let loose, the dogs immediately ran to their flat on the ground floor happily. She opened the door to the flat, the dogs rushed to their water, and her own thirst was quenched as they drank. As she was watching them she remembered the envelope in the mailbox.

Surprised at how quickly she had forgotten it she left her bag, took the house key in her hand, she went out of the locked door of the building, and walked towards the mailboxes directly on the right of the entrance between the locked door and the unlocked door. She collected the envelope from mailbox number five with its broken lock, and just as she was about to turn round, towards the locked door, she saw it, the miserable dog. It was moping, wandering in front of their block, as if it was waiting for something, perhaps a miracle. She went out through the unlocked door and approached the dog. 'Are you hungry then, what are you doing here?' she asked softly, moving slowly in order not to frighten it. The dog was not as nervous as some stray dogs that had suffered violence at human hands, and as far as she could see from the half-hopeful look in its eyes it had not been on the streets for such a long time. The dog came to her somewhat tentatively but wagging its tail. Taking a closer look, she could see that it was in a more miserable condition than she had thought in the morning. She stopped. The dog wagged its tail again. She was touched deep within. She was so touched that her ears filled up with the screams of all the living creatures that were in pain in the world. She was so touched within that she thought she would collapse and not be able to get up again. For a moment she thought about going home and bringing something to eat but she was afraid that the dog might just wander off. 'Come!' she said to the dog, and the dog went. She walked a little more, 'come!' she said again, and the dog went again. She decided on a plan. If she could take the dog to the vet that was just a few streets ahead she could have it treated there. Then might it be run over by a car, or perhaps it wouldn't, or it might fight with other stray dogs and get fatally wounded, or perhaps it wouldn't, but at least it would get rid of the worms and mites that were eating him up inside. Once it was rid of them it would certainly find something to eat in the garbage dumps of Istanbul.

The dog followed her to the vet, slightly tentative on one hand and hoping that there might be something good at the end of it on the other hand, but it did not want to come in through the garden gates. You keep it busy and I'll get something to eat, she told the boy that came out to the door; while the boy kept the dog busy she went in and took a packet of dog biscuits from the lowest shelf. She opened it in a hurry and gave it a biscuit, which the dog ate gladly but slowly. She gave it another one. As she was giving it the third, she tried to pull the dog into the garden, but the dog wasn't having it. The young veterinary nurse tugged at the dog a little bit, and the dog did not play hard to get, obviously it had nothing better to do; so it went in. The dog, although it looked very hungry, kept wagging its tail as she fed it with biscuits. By the sixth or seventh biscuit they had passed through the garden and entered the surgery when the young vet emerged from the back room, where she'd been breaking her fast. She told the woman that she wanted to have this dog treated. It was then that she found out that it could both be mites and blood worms that were eating this miserable dog up. If it was blood worms and they had infested this poor dog a long time ago there might not be anything that could be done, but if it was mange it could be treated.

The veterinarian brought an anti-mange injection from the back room and injected the dog as a precaution. As the injection burned the dog was surprised, it was scared, and with a slight wailing it hid itself behind the cashier, close to the wall. Then suddenly the woman realized that dog felt comfortable there. She felt the dog would stay there if it was allowed. But it couldn't stay. According to what the vet said, they could not take it into their lodgings because they didn't know what was wrong with it; whatever its illness was it could pass it on to the other dogs. The woman who took it there was not sure anyway; she wasn't sure she could take the responsibility of imprisoning a dog that was used to roaming the streets freely. In a sense she was relieved that she hadn't had to choose. At the back of her mind, her conscience weakly said: 'So what is going to happen?'. She shut her ears.

They got the dog out of the shop and later out of the garden by enticing it with food as they had done earlier, and with a bit of pushing and shoving. I know one shot will be of no use, but if you see it around here please give it its treatment, I'll pay for it, said the woman to the vet as she was leaving. When they went out of the garden they were alone: she and the dog. She stopped. What if it comes home with me, I can't take it inside the house, what am I going to do, she thought. The people in the building don't mind our dogs, but they surely won't want such a diseased dog around, she thought. Again she stood there not knowing what to do, the last few biscuits left in the pack in her hand; to top it all, this time even her conscience wouldn't talk to her. 'Come,' she said to the dog half-heartedly; what she really wanted was for the dog to hang around there, for the woman at the vet to give it as many injections as was necessary and feed it. She was going to pay for it, whatever the cost. I would have taken it in if I didn't have two dogs, it would have lived with us, but there is no room for it in our tiny flat. Besides both the young one and the older one would be very jealous, it would be the end of our peaceful life at home, it's not only our flat, we don't have room for it in our lives either, she thought and was disgusted with herself.

Because she was ashamed of herself, she coaxed the dog again, this time with a more determined tone. The dog did not move. 'Come!' she said again, but again the dog would not move. She could not pretend she was not happy. It was going to be much easier this way, passing the buck onto others. She was going to pay for it, whatever the cost. They were vets; the treatment could easily be continued as long as the dog hung around there. And she won't have abandoned the dog in the streets with its mange and its blood worms. The dog did not follow her. As she walked home she spaced out the dog biscuits on the side of the pavement regularly; so that people would not tread on them as they walked by and the dog would find them if it wanted to. She placed the final biscuit at the doorway of the building, and she went in with her feelings all muddled up.

She came across the dog again the next morning as she went out of her flat at half past five to go on holiday with her husband and her two dogs. The dog started joyfully wagging its tail when it saw the woman. It started walking towards her slowly, a little shyly. Her little dog, which was very jealous, immediately started growling and barking. Her older dog quietly fluffed up. An ache in her heart, she stopped. She looked at the dog from behind the door. She could not go out with her own dogs. Her dogs might kick up a fuss, but more importantly, if it had something catching she wouldn't want it to be passed onto her own dogs. She felt sick. She stopped. She opened the inner door and the three of them went back into their flat despite having left it a few minutes before. Because her young dogs ate special anti-allergenic food, she poured a cup of the older dog's food into a plastic container. Thinking they were going to have food her dogs set about doing their dance of joy: her young dog put her front paws up as high as possible and yelped, her older dog ran around, spun around itself and then stopped and looked up at her face.

Angry at the joy of her dogs, she went out of the house to their surprised looks. The miserable dog had not gone away – it was waiting in front of the outside door. It started to wag its tail with joy when it saw the food in her hand. The woman put the food on the pavement on the side of the building where she waited for a taxi to go to work each morning. The dog set about eating happily. While it was eating, she quickly went back to her house and picked up her surprised dogs, and the three of them went to her husband who had been waiting for them in the car. As soon as she opened the rear door her dogs – afraid to death of not going with mum and dad and being left behind – jumped into the car (as they always did) forgetting both the food and the stray dog that impertinently wagged its tail to their mother. Her husband started the car. They went out of the parking lot as the miserable dog was still eating its food (and how slowly it ate, that food would have been devoured a thousand times by then if it had been her own monsters).

All through the holiday her heart ached whenever she thought of that stray dog which she had sloppily tried to adopt, with its mange and blood worms or whatever it had. It even occurred to her that it might still be around. I wonder if it'll be there when we go back, she hoped and feared at the same time.

They came back at noon two days later. The dog was not to be seen. Perhaps it'll come in the evening, she thought; but the dog did not come. She looked around the next morning as she was going to work, but the dog was not there. She called the vet when she came home towards evening: no, they hadn't seen the dog either. Perhaps it will appear again, she said to herself, half-heartedly hoping, not knowing what she would do when the dog appeared: how she would take it to the vet regularly and have it treated, how she would bring herself to leave the dog on its own in the street and go back inside her house full of warmth, food and water while the dog looked at her with half hopeful eyes. The dog did not appear again. For animals can tell who is sincere and who is not.

The Bite

How happy I was that summer. We had moved from a flat into a house with a huge garden. The garden was so big I couldn't be bothered to run all the way down it. There were trees in the back, I love trees. The beach was also very close, and my mother often took me to the beach. Then we would take a shower in the garden, then mum would give me a bone, and I would lie at her feet drowsily chewing at it. There were two *Alsatians* and a *Golden Retriever* living next door, I used to bark at them behind the fence whenever I felt like it. Mum was glad I barked at them; because I hadn't barked at anyone until then. As a matter of fact, I used to bark at them for the sake of it; as we didn't go hunting or anything, you know, I didn't have much to do. Since mum enjoyed it, though, I decided I would bark whenever I got a chance.

As dad often went on trips we were on our own with mum most of the time. I like dad very much as well but I like being with mum when he is gone even better. Then I could loll on the side dad sleeps. Mum, if she happens to wake up at night, sees me near her, and holds me and kisses me on my nose. That is how our days went by, more or less like this.

Until she came.

One day, mum was at the garden gate, with a tiny, dark and puny thing in her hand. A dog! Who asked me? I was extremely annoyed. I lowered my ears and looked at mum expressively, as I always did when I was annoyed, I made a noise of discontent and turned my tail on her and the thing she was holding and sat down. And it was at that moment that I understood things would not be the same again from then on. Normally mum couldn't have suffered this move for more than ten seconds, she would have rushed by me immediately, apologized for whatever she did to hurt me, put her face close to me so that I would lick her, and make beautiful noises from her throat like those she'd learnt from me. Normally I couldn't but give way when she did that; I would give her a big lick right away. But what's that! Mum isn't even aware that I am out of sorts! She's kissing and cuddling the thing on her lap. Dad was at home as well that day. He came downstairs upon mum's call. And if mum hasn't also tied a red ribbon on that black creature's neck! Oh God, comprendo? This dog is not a guest or anything; it's clearly a gift for dad! It's going to be with us forever. Now we're done for.

This time dad took it. And what a spoilt thing it was! What a tart, all that tail-swaying. Creep!

Ha! At least don't bother me, right, I'm obviously sulking here. Sidling up close, going over and under me, what's all this? Much too familiar for my liking... I'll take it from mum, but from no one else. I'll keep my distance even from dad. But still you can see this unwelcome dog is constantly pestering me.

And I mean constantly pestering me! I'm going to go nuts. You don't tread upon someone's heels when they're peeing man! Let me pee peacefully, girl, will you! Little fool! Anyway, she understood that she should keep out from under my feet when I'm peeing when she got a dozen litres of pee on her head. Well, she shouldn't have stood where I was peeing should she!

What a nuisance. I lie down, and there she is beside me. When I walk, she'll be crushed if I'm not careful, she is one tenth of my size, after all. I sit down and she gets on my back. The shrew.

Still there's hope. Maybe she'll stay a few more days and then go. Then... what's that! If she didn't settle herself on the bed from the first night! Now see that mother of mine! Leave her down there, the brat couldn't climb up to the bed. If she didn't just pick her up and take her in her bosom. So she was a tiny baby, she needed love very much, she was taken from her mother too soon and she grew up without a mother all this time, hearing heartbeats calmed her down. Well, the bed is crowded. I behave politely and curl up at mum's feet, then I see this little hussy is in her bosom. Now that is too much.

That was all we needed; missy's ruined our night's sleep as well. The so-called baby, she suddenly lets it go on the bed (girl, I was two months old when I learnt how to hold it). Ah, man! Get up, change the sheets! If mum wakes up just before she releases it and understands that she needs to go, (the idiot can't jump down either), she picks her up in her arms, takes her out onto the balcony, missy pees, and she steps on her pee as well, the balcony is cleaned, the paws are cleaned in the middle of the night, and then back into mum's arms, cuddling again... No, that is too much for me.

I told them so, but who would hear me. None of my sulking worked. Mum is not stupid, she was well aware that I didn't want this dog but she was trying to trick me into it. 'Look, when she grows up she'll keep you company when we're not at home, then maybe she'll be a beautiful girl and you'll get married, you'll have puppies if you like;' puppies or no puppies, what do I care. 'But I still love my boy very much he's my darling, you're my darling my big dog where's my baby here mummy's got you your favourite milky bone,' says she and I'm fooled. I say I've grown up but I too am like a child. Show me a bone and I'm hers. One day, two days, three days.

Then one morning I saw mum had packed her suitcase. I looked in her eyes with my saddest face again. 'You'll wait for mummy a little while and she'll come,' said mum. When she says that, she doesn't come back for at least a few days. Leaving me at home with this little creep, shame on you.

And see that father of mine! He's literally crazy about this thing. He doesn't cuddle me like that much, even though I am a male and I don't really like cuddles, but he doesn't let this girl off his lap. Oh, let them do whatever they want; all the better. Let this dark thing be dad's and leave mum to me. When is mum coming?

One day. Two days. Three days. Ah, there's mum! She's turned round the corner, the sound of her car, her smell. Oh, how I've missed her, let me draw the smell in a bit. I got up at once and rushed to the garden gate. What's that! Who's that racing over jumping from dad's high lap in a commando jump! It's the imposed family member! Hey missy, as if you've been in the house long enough to miss mother! You've only been with us for three weeks! You just dare try jumping on mum; you'll get what's coming to you.

Anyway, mum was the mother I knew. She missed me more. Ah, kiss me on the jowl too. Ah, scratch my backside too. Wait let me lie down the way you like with my paws up. Yes, bite me on my chin too you love it! Hey! What's it with you, move it! You go to your father, you latecomer!

My happiness was short-lived. Apparently mum petted me first so that I wouldn't be jealous. Then she took the thing in her arms. Rub and cuddle. For minutes! I think I'm going to throw up.

Now how about that! Whose idea was it to put these food bowls side by side? Wasn't she eating in the kitchen? Are we supposed to eat together with this thing now? That's great. You'll see if I don't just walk off.

Mum put out food for both of us. Restlessly, I keep checking what she's eating as well. Her food smells nicer. Mum has realized something is wrong; she's trying to soothe me. She's a puppy Goldie, her food is puppy food. I'm going to give my boy a big bone in a minute. It all happened as I was trying to let mum know with my eyes how pleased I was to hear the word bone. The puppy had sidled up in such a way that I didn't see it. Seeing her head over my bowl, and I was kind of angry anyway, I happened to open my jaws by a sudden reflex. I suddenly saw that mum was screaming and shouting. Just as I was saying, wait what are you so frightened of, I realized that there was blood dripping on my food bowl from Blackie's head: I had bitten her. Oh dear, now I don't understand how it happened at all. When did my teeth ever sink into that tiny head of hers. You can clearly see the bone. What's more, I've made mother cry too. But amazingly she didn't get angry with me, not at all. She just grabbed her bag in a hurry, took Blackie in her arms, rushed to the garden gate and went out. They got into the car and went.

An hour went by, no sign of them. Two hours went by, no sign of them. Three hours went by, no sign of them. What should I do, should I call dad? Mum turned the corner of the street as I was brooding on it. There's still one minute and six seconds for her to come home. How am I going to bear it? God knows, I've been eating my heart out for hours. Is she awfully mad at me? Did she leave without saying anything because she was very angry with me? and here she comes. I can't tell you how happy I was, my tail nerves were about to break off their roots for joy. Mum got out of the car, she opened the garden gate. I jumped on her and gave her a big lick. In fact, it appears I over did it a bit, I was about to make her fall. But to tell you the truth, it would never have occurred to me that my eyes would search for that little thing. Had I killed the little girl or what? Oh God, I'm a murderer, and so young too!

Mum saw it. She saw that I was worried. She always answers me when I look at her questioningly. I tilt my head to the left and look deep into her eyes. Don't worry you big lump, everything is all right, mummy loves you very much, she said.

Blackie? She's fit as a fiddle. She's healthier than you or me. Perhaps she wouldn't be smacking my ears so if she knew I was the cause of the stitches on her head. Cut it out girl, you're tickling me!

REVENGE

Iraq I

Our father hated us, especially me. Perhaps because my sister Raghad's face resembled his, sometimes he looked like he could stand her but I'm sure he hated me from the moment I was born. You can tell when your mother or father hates you.

I hated my father. I hated him all my life, patiently, every day, every minute. Every night I prayed tirelessly for him to die, and to die in agony. It took him too long to die.

Our father was most fond of Uday. Newspapers reported that he loved our youngest sister Hala as well – wherever they got the idea from. That is not true. He only loved one son. And he did not care for Hala, not at all.

Uday outdid his father in sadism and perversion; *his* death was the doing of the Americans just like his father's. I did not shed a tear. Perhaps all those lives he took so cruelly, whipped, electrocuted, and slashed were avenged if only a little bit.

So Uday was not good but Qusay was? Never. He too was both a sadist and a pervert, like all the men in the family; and sly to boot. When Uday fell out of favour because of his cruelty and those hashish parties, Qusay threw himself even more fiercely into the ranks of the secret service, proud to be the clever and dutiful child. Idiot! As if our father could love any one of his children other than Uday, in whom he saw himself, whom he saw as himself. The American boys did away with him and Uday, at the same time, in Mosul. God has his ways.

My husband Saddam Kamil Hassan al-Majid and his brother were good men. Of course my father had forced us – my sister and me – to marry these two brothers. Nevertheless, we were as happy as we could have been. But it did not last. He had our husbands killed as soon as we returned to Iraq from exile. Gullible fools that we were. My father had granted a pardon, so to say, and his one and only son Uday had guaranteed that nothing would happen. 'Come back from exile. It is true you have drifted apart from us but we have pardoned you now, come,' they said. Like fools, we went back to Iraq only to witness the death of our husbands. We swallowed this story, as if our father had a heart that could be offended or that would pardon, as if he had a bit of conscience. God damn him. God damn him ever more. Damn him in the after life too.

'We were proud of his courage when he came face to face with his executor at the end of the rope,' his spokesman told the newspapers. We were proud that he did not have his face covered, that he did not tremble as the noose was passed over his head. Lies. It's all a bunch of lies. That American commander, the one I told where my father was hiding, is my witness. He died begging.

Open Up! Police!

Such commotion on Imbros these days... they're buying the old houses and mending them, painting them, and decorating them. It's as if the island is getting ready for a wedding we locals don't know about! There is no end to the number of Istanbul licence plates that come and go. 'Just wait and see how it is going to get so very expensive around here soon, heaven forbid that a place get in the hands of Istanbul residents,' I say to Hüseyin, the grocer. 'Çeşme, Adatepe, Tenedos; so it's our turn now, let's get this humble house into shape a little and sell it,' I say, but he doesn't care the least bit.

Hüseyin didn't care but I set to work at the house in the town centre, it had been standing there destitute ever since Pa died. We'd better get down to work before it's too late, I said to myself, a buyer might suddenly come up, you never know!

One day in early summer, when I was with the men I had hired to put the house into shape, somebody kept calling my name: 'Abdülrahman Bey, Abdülrahman Bey!'. I looked up and saw a youngish couple. 'What is it, guys?' I asked. I didn't know them and they didn't look familiar either. It turned out that they were interested in my brother-in-law's two-storey house in Kaleköy. My brother-in-law is in Germany, but my name is in the advert. The young ones weren't dressed so well either but I had to see to them. We jumped into my old banger and went to have a look. I showed them around the house. Well, the amount my brother is asking for is not so much but the house needs gutting. As soon as I had named the price I understood that these guys couldn't afford to have this house repaired and licked into shape. The girl loved the place; apparently she loved living in such highlands. Their house in Istanbul was in the inner city, she couldn't see any mountains when she looked outside. Whereas the town she was born in was mountainous, it was green; she's been missing the mountains ever since she came to study in Istanbul. To tell you the truth, I didn't listen to it all, but I liked the little thing when she proudly said 'I'm a lawyer' at the end of her speech! I mean she said it with such pride.

'Come, let me offer you some tea at our Kurdish place up there,' I said.

'Fine,' they said and followed me.

There was no one in the tent and the door to the kitchen was closed too. I knocked, 'Uncle Mahmut!' I called out as loud as I could because he is hard of hearing. But we could hear no sound from inside. The young man banged on the door and shouted 'Open up! Police!'- just for fun. Oh boy... you have no idea; this is no laughing matter. You don't know boy, at night, when you're fast asleep in your bed that is how those men bang at your door; just like you did. If you don't open up, well, the bullets could hit anywhere. You're bound to open up, boy. While your wife is shaking like a leaf, and your daughters, with their heads down for fear, don't know where to hide themselves. They won't even let you get dressed. Sneak a glance at your wife. There is no hope in those eyes. There is no hope in your eyes. This is the fourth visit to that dark cell, and there might be no getting out. You might be pushed to suicide, hanging yourself with a blanket. You might hear them say, we did not take your husband, fuck off, or else we'll bring your daughters. You might be lost. You might be thrown in front of your house riddled with bullets. You might be found inside a well, years later: So many mights. And so there is no hope.

If there is God up there – at least for your wife, but there is no God when you are electrocuted through your balls. There is no God when all that can be done with a truncheon is practised on you. There is no God when your knees break noisily from the kicks they receive. There is no God, just men with masks, men with gloves, men with truncheons. There is only a lifeless light, dripping water and shouts from the next cell. You cannot distinguish between recorded shouts and real ones; besides, it does not matter. If the cell next door is empty that day, what's on tape is real. Don't joke, boy. This is not a matter to joke about. My blood freezes as you continue the joke, but how am I supposed to explain it to you?

What words shall I find and produce for you with my tongue; this tongue that has had salt rubbed into so many times. How my wife cried and kissed each purple, each red, and each broken part one by one every time I was thrown in front of the door. You can't put this into words. The tongue goes silent the eye does not, boy. The eye does not forget. See, your chatty wife understood that I am moved to tears. She doesn't look like she's ever seen a cell, but it's evident she was moved to tears for some reason at one time. While you were still childishly hitting the door I moved closer to her and showed her my knees. She'd been observing my limping the whole time. 'Ali,' I said. 'The policeman's called Ali. He retired last year; he owns the *LookLittleTasteMuch* chocolates now'.

Batman

'Why are there so many suicide cases in Batman?' they ask. What else is there to do if you cannot avenge yourself but with your own life?

I was going to take Hamdiye as my wife. So she was fifteen years my senior, so she joined the organization, so who knows whose mistress she had become within the organization, that didn't bother me at all. I loved Hamdiye. 'Why did Hamdiye join the organization,' they ask. 'She's a traitor,' they say, 'and she's defiled to boot'. What else is there but to run away or to die if you give her no other choice than to marry a randy sixty-year-old when she is only twelve? The rope waits to be passed over somebody's neck. The mountains howl like hungry wolves.

They say Hamdiye walked from one mountain to another, destitute, for fourteen years. But she couldn't bear the cold or the cruelty, so she came down and surrendered. She gave away a few important names, her sentence was commuted, and she was imprisoned for a while and then released. I happened to come across her on the day she was released. It was after school, at my father's shop. She'd missed watermelons most when she was inside. She had come to buy a watermelon. When she saw the uniform I was wearing she looked at it enviously, I figured she had wanted to go to school but couldn't. What grade are you in, she asked me. Oh, the beating of my heart! She asked that question with a smile in her dark eyes. If she only knew the fire she started within me! 'It's my final year in senior high school,' I said. 'How nice, well done,' she said. Her hair in the front had gone slightly grey. She had wrinkles around her eyes, but the dimple on her left cheek, the darkness of her hair, the darkness of her eyes, ah! I've never seen such a beauty in all my short life.

She made me choose the watermelon – 'just pick one,' she said. I picked the choicest. I wouldn't let her pay. She insisted.

'I can't accept that; I won't take it,' I said.

Just as she was about to turn round and leave having said, thank you, take care, I couldn't resist it, I shouted like a child: 'I'm going to take you as my wife!'

'What did you just say?' she asked as she turned round, her dimple looking at me at the same time.

'Are you married,' I asked.

She sighed. 'I'm not,' she said.

'Good, I'll take you as my wife then,' I said. '

They won't let you near me honey, I'm probably twice your age, isn't there someone young you love,' she said. 'Look, I've just been released from prison, your family won't want me,' she said.

Seeing I wouldn't take any of it, she added 'I was in the organization for fourteen years'. I shrugged. I curled my lip. Seeing it was stubbornness in me she walked away murmuring, crazy boy.

I wouldn't let her go, though. I asked around and found out where she lived. Her father had died, and her mother, nearing the end of her life, had forgiven her daughter. Three sisters and a mother, they lived in a two-room house. Every day, I went every day, after school, and waited in front of her door. She grew accustomed to me... 'Crazy boy, you're leading me astray, we have no future, you're going to get yourself in trouble,' she said; I didn't listen. 'My mother and father will understand me,' I said. Didn't my mother elope with my father when they were young, they know what love is.

But it seems they don't! They knew nothing but selfishness! Mum was furious when she heard I was in love with someone fifteen years older than me. A terrorist, and defiled to boot! She yelled and screamed, 'we said it was our only son, we went without food but fed you, we went without clothes but dressed you, are you going to bring trouble on our family now, get out of my sight!' When my father came home in the evening they talked in the living room, whispering. A few minutes later my father stormed into my room and came at me calling me a cuckold. He lathered me. 'You'll get the fuck out of this house if I ever hear that girl's name again!' he said.

Well, haven't I got them in the newspapers and disgraced them now! Haven't I left them without a son, without an heir! Haven't I done what my Hamdiye could not do years ago! Have I not avenged myself on my mother, who eloped with the man she loved but did not give me to the one I loved, and cursed the women of this place saying, how could they themselves take away the life that God has given, with a wispy rope hung from the ceiling!

Child

She never once called me by my name. Child this, child that...

My own mother was taken away by the military police one night and we did not see her after that. I was nine. Men don't cry but I cried once. My father saw me crying clinging on to our black hen's neck. He beat me purple. He screamed his head off saying, your mum was a whore what are you crying after her for.

Seems mum had loved a soldier. His commander had forbidden him to see her. Where I come from soldiers don't like us. But these two had continued seeing each other in secret. My aunt told me all about it one night. Until then, I had thought mum was taken away because she had aided my uncle who was up at the mountains*. Many a time she had told my uncle to come down, to surrender, but my uncle could not. He had tried running away a few times but each time they had tied him to a rock and deprived him of food and water for days. Mum couldn't find it in her heart to abandon her brother, so she used to send him this and that now and then.

Apparently that was not why they took her away. It's not that I didn't go crazy when I heard about it. I would have given her a good slap if she were near me. But she wasn't; mum had long since gone, so what would it matter if I were angry, if I went mad? I was curious too, so I bowed my head down and listened.

Back then, before long, their affair had reached my father's ears. And my father was so bloody-minded. He spied on my mother for ten whole days without uttering a word. Finally, when he saw it with his own eyes, he decided to take revenge. He knew that if he shot her he would be done for himself... and he likes his comfort. He couldn't do time in jail or anything. So he decided it would be best to go the gendarmes. He turned up at the door of

---

* Going up to the mountains means joining the PKK, a terrorist organisation fighting for an independent Kurdish state

the station. The gendarmes were only too pleased; they had been looking forward to mum turning out to be a traitor so that they could take her in, because my uncle was up at the mountains; because my grandfather would not pay tribute to the village guard. 'This traitor is sending provisions to her brother,' said my father.

They came and took mum away one night. They didn't even let her put her headscarf on; she went just like that, bareheaded and barefoot, in the middle of the night. I was nine. My siblings were sleeping. Mum entrusted my siblings in my care, so she must have known she wasn't coming back. Two days went by, nothing. My father left the children with me and went to the station. It turned out he had known, he had expected it; they'd killed her. My mother was six months pregnant when they took her. She was beaten black and blue, and passed away in the night, her babe still inside. After that day my father forbade us from asking about our mother. 'Your mother is dead,' he said. 'She is not to be asked about, her name is not to be mentioned, there will be no crying. Otherwise I'll beat you to death'.

After just over a year, there came the stepmother. She is from the neighbouring village. Let it be a young and beautiful one while we're at it, thought my father, and he went and brought in a fifteen-year-old girl. She soon fell pregnant. What airs and graces. When my mother was pregnant she would go to the field, cook food, and look after us. You can't get near this one for all her airs and graces. And never mind all that, I was not a child any more! I was a man. I was eleven. This is my house! I know what to do with you and with your husband who backs you.

I gave her a thrashing when she was exactly six months pregnant like mum was. So what if she's older than me – mine is the strength of a man. May she never give birth!

Girl Child

It's my cousin. He's made mincemeat out of the woman. He turned up at the hotel one evening. I was at the reception making up a receipt. He was drunk. His eyes were bloodshot. Hide me, he said. I didn't ask why – he's come to both my aid and my father's many times. The car overheats, we call him. We have an accident, we call him; I don't know, that sort of thing. When we run into trouble he is the first person that comes to our mind. I didn't ask. I got him into one of the dorms in the basement. He was terrified too... I was afraid. It took all I had to ask, so that I would know what to protect him from, praying silently to God that he hadn't killed anyone, although, if that were the case, God forbid, we would still have dealt with it; one of my cousins had accidently run over a child that had suddenly jumped in front of him once and my father had settled the issue by giving money and so on to the child's family: Blood is thicker than water. We protect our family name. I couldn't wait for his answer: 'Did you kill someone brother?' I asked. I beat up a woman,' he said. 'But I beat the prostitute up bad, she blew my top,' he said. 'Seems she went to the police. They'll be here in a few minutes, the police knew I'd come to the hotel,' he said. Ours is a big city but everybody knows one another. And if you are a man of property you see...

I went up to the lobby straight away. I went into my office. The police arrived just as I was about to have a cup of coffee. They had told the security to call their boss outside. I went out. There was a woman inside the police car, but her face was crumpled up like paper. You know how you crumple up a can of cola with both of your hands, like that. 'This guy beats up his wife as well but he's actually made mincemeat out of that woman. She was a prostitute. This lady has filed a complaint against your cousin,' said the policeman. I played surprised: 'Well. I haven't seen my cousin for days,' I said. 'Are you certain he did this, I'm not saying this because he's my cousin but I've never seen him do any wrong, I've never heard of anything against him, he is a very decent man,' I said. I hoped they'd buy it. They weren't going to bust the hotel and search it; they know to keep their distance.

The policeman made some feeble objections but it takes guts to step inside without a search warrant. 'Please let us know if he comes to you,' he said. 'Certainly officer' I said. To tell you the truth, even though I was dying to take a look at the woman's face, I couldn't bring myself to do it.

I went downstairs to see my cousin as soon as the police were gone. He had dozed off. I called his wife. 'Sister, my buddy was over here, we drank a little too much, he fell asleep, don't worry, he's going to stay at the hotel tonight,' I said. She didn't suspect anything. Although, what would it matter if she had, what could she say.

The next morning I woke up a bit worried. I found some time before the operations meeting and told my sister about the case – what the hell made me tell her, why the hell did I ever tell her? The fury, oh the fury! 'And what else was I supposed to do, was I supposed to hand my own cousin in to the police?' I asked. She flew off the handle. She uttered some of those well known words of hers. The tribe spirit, she said, the macho culture and so on. 'We're in for it,' I said, at this time in the morning. This was all we needed. She grumbled on and on, her eyes filled with tears for rage, and then she buggered off, hang the meeting.

My cousin woke up towards noon. I asked him to stay for breakfast, he didn't. I sent him home with one of the cars. I don't know what kind of a lie he came up with for his wife about his swollen hands and scratched face.

I didn't even think about that event again. It didn't occur to me, I forgot about it. Until last year; until my wife gave birth to a teeny-weeny baby last year, the sweetest little girl. Was it that I became more sensitive because I became a father or what? Ever since then, the crumpled face of that woman, who was herself a teeny-weeny baby girl once, has been haunting me in my dreams. I wake up and can't go to sleep again.

My Brother

The three of them suddenly came into my room one night. I saw that my favourite brother, the youngest of my big brothers, had a cable in his hand! He wrapped it around my throat before I could ask what was going on. He started tightening it. He was crying at the same time. My eldest brother was like a stone, staring at me. I was sad not because I was going to die but because this job fell to the youngest of my big brothers. Although he was the one that loved me most, that protected me most, they laid it on him because he was underage. Poor kind-hearted brother of mine; how could you be taken in by their words and have the heart to kill me?

My death came quickly and quietly but I was undaunted. Ever since my first night in the next world I haunted my eldest brother's dreams every night, persistently each night, until reports appeared in the newspapers. He turned out to be stronger than I expected; after all, he's the one that is most like his father. But nine years is a long time, he couldn't stand it.

Yesterday, he finally went to the police and blurted it all out: 'We killed our sister!' While they tried to make sure I wouldn't be the talk of the neighbourhood they themselves appeared in the newspapers altogether as family, serves them right! 'I didn't know anything about it. I didn't know they were going to kill her. I was the last person to find out,' said my father. Don't believe him. He's the one who had me strangled.

Expert in Filth

You did well to call me in, Inspector. Don't consider this as self-conceit but I'm a real *Expert in Filth*. I understand whether they're filthy or not from the way they enter the room, from the way they say hello, from the way they sit or cannot sit, from the way they look or cannot look me in the eye.

I just saw the child's father; your officers provided an opportunity for us to talk. I know you're praying inside that I would tell you something good, but you're not going to like what I'm going to say. Are you all torn up because the child is just three years old, only three? Have we not seen seventeen-month-old ones, Inspector? You shrink inside your majestic uniform, inside your huge body, like a five-year-old child, you're afraid of what you're going to hear from me. Perhaps you're cursing your work, which condemns you to witnessing all of this. Yet none of that is going to help you hurt less inside for what I am going to tell you. If you like, come and see me on Monday, we'll see if we can ease your soul. Your work is nothing like those American films in which they drink a lot of coffee and show off, right? Mine is not a feast either but what can one do? I chose to be an *Expert in Filth* myself. Somebody has to do the job. For Inspector, it does not matter whether they are seventeen months old, or three or five, or girls or boys: Behind some walls there is so much filth that tonnes of bleach could not wash them clean. What I mean to say is don't be taken in by the so-called bursts of rage, the passionate oaths for vengeance, the floods of tears. The sleep of some mothers is somehow always deep, and the fathers of some houses are always strangers.

Betrayal

Womenkind, right, birdbrains, the lot of them... Man, like I won't find somewhere to grab her by if she doesn't have her hair... Is her hair all I've got? For God's sake. They're all birdbrains and ingrates to boot! What's the older one done? She's gone and reported it to the newspapers. Is this what one should do to her own father! Why, come to me and we'll talk; I'll tell you why and what for. Their mother was the same. Ingrate. They've both taken after her. But especially the older one... that older one, that stubborn mule... that pig... that wicked girl... that. But I'm cleverer than her! Write this down pal: You know that shopping centre that was bombed ten years ago... the one in Mahmutpaşa? Right, well, the bomber is my elder daughter Sema. I have my evidence too, I'm going to hand it all in to the police one by one. She'll see now what it means to betray a father. Write it exactly in those words.

Baby Girl

This is what they wrote at the end of the news report: 'In India, especially among the poor uneducated families, daughters are seen as a burden and are killed.'

The police thought it was the doing of another family that wanted to get rid of their baby that came out a girl instead of a boy. That is what first comes to mind amongst our people here. It would have been more acceptable if that had been the history of the two-day-old girl baby that came out alive from under the ground in Hyderabad; for there are many cases of that. When by some miracle the baby was found, the police lost no time to start investigating around the village. It was not difficult to locate the new born girl babies, and with a bit of threatening and interrogation they saw that Meryem's daughter was missing and immediately arrested the baby's grandfather Rahman, her mother Meryem, and her father Hüseyin.

Meryem... Oh, Meryem! Why wouldn't you marry me Meryem! You'd promised, remember? Remember you wrapped your arms around me with joy flowing from your black eyes when I said I didn't care if you gave birth to ten daughters! Remember you'd said, I won't look at anyone else then, I'll marry you! How happily you'd gone home that day, your eyes glittering with the fresh beauty of nine years of age, thinking you'd found a man who would accept you with your daughters. It's not easy, exactly three of your sisters had been strangled before your eyes, you were the lucky one; they didn't have the heart to kill you because you were their firstborn.

I waited until you were fifteen. That is what your father had said; I won't give her before she's fifteen, he'd said. For six years, from when I was eighteen, when I saw you and fell in love with you, till I was twenty-four, I didn't turn my head to look if it were a she bird that was passing by. I thought of you every hour, every minute. I dreamt of that blessed day on which you'd be my bride. I dreamt of it this way and that. I dressed you and undressed you many a time. I made us a house, we had ten daughters but I didn't love any of them more than I loved you. It didn't occur to me for a day that I should have a son. I took such good care of you that the wives of the neighbours turned green with envy as they fell to pieces, endlessly beaten up every night. I neither touched a single hair on your head nor did I ever, not on a single night, take you if you didn't feel like it. We were so happy Meryem! I dreamt of you in many ways, in all sorts of ways. I knew you better than myself. On the day you turn fifteen I'll take you away from your father's house, then we'll have a family as large as you wish, however you like... I used to say.

For all those years, did I not understand at all that you weren't in love with me! Oh Meryem! Did I not realize at all that your heart belonged to someone else? So you loved Prabhakar all this time and not me. What about the eyes you made at me as you passed by our shop? What about those sweet smiles? What about your appearing in my dreams every single night?! Does it matter that we didn't ever talk about our nuptial again after that day! Hadn't we promised each other! My word is my word, it seems yours was not!

I did it out of love Meryem. I did it out of love. But you see I couldn't even manage that! The idiot that I am! I'm going to turn myself in now; I can't bear to hurt you. I can bear to hurt your daughter but I can't bear to hurt you. Don't end up in prison Meryem. Don't end up in prison. I'm to blame for this, Meryem. I'm going to tell the police now. As a wretched man who hasn't even been able to avenge himself, I deserve to die anyway.

Soul Raiser

When you wake up without reason and feel a slight breeze over your head, that is me.

As you open your eyes, shaken as if you were falling off a cliff, I am right at your ear.

If, in your dream, there is a knock on the door and you wake up, and if there is a knock on the door at your house and there is no one there, that is me.

If you are having terrible nightmares, if a diabolic incubus is plaguing you, if you open your eyes in the middle of the night unable to breathe, I am there on top of you.

If you are turning right and left for no reason, if you drift off for a few minutes and then wake up again with bloodshot eyes from sleeplessness, that is me.

If your door is creaking for no reason, if your quiet fridge has suddenly started to work noisily, if the walls are expanding and the curtains are rustling, I am in your house.

If you suddenly wake up from your sleep at its sweetest point, shivering inside in the middle of summer, that is me.

If you want to scream in your dream and you have no voice, if you have understood that is a dream only after I have told you, know that in fact you are very close to death.

If nobody's lights are out in the street but yours is, if a groundless radiance is filtered through your window in that silent darkness, that is my cruel light.

I raise souls every night.

For I know not sleep myself.

The Leg

I recognized my leg. Anyone would recognize their own leg. You would, if it was put up on auction on the Internet. You would, even if it were in a gold plated, Swarovski-encrusted, elegant ice bucket.

You'd think such things only happened in new-fangled cheap thrillers: you wake up from your sleep and your leg is gone. It could have been the work of the organ mafia that kidnaps children for spleens, kidneys and hearts if it were not a leg but a spleen, a kidney, or a heart or something. But your right leg having vanished when you wake up in your own bed one morning? Now, you don't expect that. Nonetheless, this actually happened to me, I who never took good care of my muscles.

I didn't know you were so spiteful. Whose stride are you going to march to now?

Chump

Remember I used to bark so, remember the quick-tempered woman next door kept complaining about me to the compound security. And mum and dad would say, 'Blackie is a puppy still, that's why she barks, she'll calm down when she grows up a little, please be patient for a while,' but I wouldn't stop barking and the woman kept on complaining... Eh, my well-meaning darling, my silly Goldie, you chump, if you only knew what a memory I've got. I was born a little spiteful as well, what can I say: Don't I know not to bark? Who's the baby, I'm a big girl already! I can hold my pee, I've learnt how to keep quiet, I'm aware of everything. Now tell me: who is it that goes to work with dad every day and has the whole day to wander about so there are no more complaints? And you, you chump, mope at home all on your own waiting for mum and dad to come back from work! Don't think Blackie doesn't know what caused the scar on her head!

CRY

Srebrenica

The water cried, the fire cried, the cloud cried, the cinders cried on eleven July. I am Srebrenica! What happened to the safeguarding of my land that was declared 'secure' by the United Nations in '93?

People flocked to me, running from the war, after I was declared secure. While I was glad for each new footstep I welcomed on the one hand, my heart fluttered with each breath on the other. For somewhere deep down I was scared inside, I have long learnt not to trust people, I am very old. My name changes yet my wisdom remains within the roots of my trees.

Now that I was secure, how the Dutch soldiers of the United Nations rushed to disarm the Bosnian Muslims! Where were your soldiers when the Serbian cannons were pounding me! Where were your soldiers when my boys and my men were packed into storehouses one by one!

You called it the greatest ethnic massacre after World War II. All right, fine, where are the culprits? – the real culprits? Where are those invincible Serbian leaders now, how well they have been hiding for all these years! How come your superpowers that find terrorists in anthills when they want failed to trace the bloody footsteps of the murderers that are all over Bosnia!

On eleven July nineteen ninety-five the heavens and the earth cried. Billions of lives sheltered on and beneath my soil shook in their boots. Neither my reptiles nor my winged animals could find themselves a place to hide. The Serbs who passed through the United Nations soldiers effortlessly and crossed through my borders packed eight thousand Bosnian men – wave after wave – into trucks and shot them in my forests. Then they crushed their corpses by bulldozers and threw them into mass graves. There were those who, at seventy-seven, could not hold their pee and also those at thirteen who were not old enough to grow a moustache yet. They say it is eight thousand but it is more than that if you ask me; I still feel their pain, I still hear their screams. Can you not hear them over there?

Jellyfish Babies

In a corner of Micronesia, we, the victims of America's nuclear energy experiments, fresh new babies not quite formed, underdone, missing something... we either fall to pieces like jelly on the operating table or we are born without limbs. Or else we are smothered in the next room before our mothers get up from their delivery beds so that they would not go crazy upon seeing what has come out of them: us freaks. Before we meet our death, however, we have all agreed to scream as loud as we can! That is all that lies in our power in those few minutes we meet life – a cry for help from beyond the ocean. Even if not for ourselves; for the sake of those to come.

I'm Not Handing Over My Wife

My name is Muhammed. I'm in love with Şehnaz. I've loved her since the first day I set eyes on her at seventeen years old. Our tribes did not allow us to get married. They wanted to marry me to my uncle's daughter and her to one of the notables of her own tribe. I abducted Şehnaz one night. We became man and wife.

Today is the fifth day of the third month we've spent in fear. Şehnaz keeps saying, my father and his people are going to find me; they're going to come and take me away. But we have no other place to go. We've taken refuge in this small village in southern Pakistan. Every day we pray that we would not be found.

Şehnaz is with child. My Şehnaz is going to give birth to a tiny baby.

Yet no matter how hard I try... I can't suppress this bad feeling I have inside.

It's been the same dream for the past three nights: Şehnaz has gone to the market to get some stuff. I'm at home as no hoeing work has come up that day. There's a knock on the door. Five men from Şehnaz's tribe, they fly at me as soon as I open the door. 'Give us Şehnaz, she's ours,' they say. 'She's my wife, I won't,' I say. 'Where is she, search the house, says the oldest'. Our house has all but two rooms; they disrupt the pillows, the mattresses and everything. It is evident Şehnaz is not at home. 'We'll wait, but first we'll deal with you,' they say. The youngest among them comes at me with a knife in his hand. Two more of them close in and hold my arms. I struggle. Not for my sake, but for what would happen to my wife and my child if I died. I scream as loud as I can. It has no effect on them. The young one cuts my ears off in one fell swoop with his knife.

My dreams come true. They're going to come and cut my ears off.

Batman

R.'s big brother was sent to prison. I was returned to my family upon my uncle's promise: 'Nobody's going to bother or touch A.N. no matter what. I assume responsibility for anything that may happen to him,' is what he wrote and gave to the prosecutor.

R. and I had been seeing each other for a year. I used to secretly go to her from Diyarbakır, to Batman. R. is a distant relative of one of our relatives. She called one day, she was crying on the phone. We've been flooded here, we've lost people from my uncle's family, come, she said. I took some of the money from under the carpet and leapt on a bus. If only my legs had broken and I had not done so.

I'd never gone near their house before. We always met far away from their house, on the hills and dales. My family would shoot us both if they heard, R. used to say. She was scared to death of her father. I asked around until I found their house. I crouched in a corner. It was crowded and there were rescue teams from Istanbul. R.s' street was not that bad after all, the water had hit the houses but it had not been able to demolish most of them. After about an hour I saw R. at the window... I was excited. I tried to wave at her, but she ran inside as soon as she'd seen me, and it seemed to me she was signalling me to go. So I tried to return, thinking that there was probably a situation and we weren't going to be able to talk. I could not.

There were seven of them altogether. Her father, her big brother, and who knows what other relatives. Seven of them.

'They'll kill me if you hand me to my family in this state. I've been dishonoured. Our family is a large one. It's a tribe. We have blood law' I said to the prosecutor.

The prosecutor did not know what to do at first. Then, seeing that I was in danger he sent me to the shelter in Batman.

I heard on my third day there that my father and folks had come to Batman; I was afraid I'd be found out. I ran away from there.

I went to the police and said, 'I wish to see the prosecutor, it's urgent'. Bless them, they were helpful. The prosecutor took the trouble and came to the precinct. It turned out my uncle was waiting outside as well. My uncle is the only person whose word I trust. 'Fine, let him come,' I said. The prosecutor called my uncle. Upon seeing him I started crying. 'I promise you, I'll shoot anyone that lays a finger on you myself,' he said. When he said so I believed him, I went back home.

They sent R.'s brother to prison, her father was released, yet this was all his doing. I called the prosecutor as soon as I'd read it in the newspaper. He'd given me his phone number saying, call me if you're in trouble. 'Why did you let her father go, he is the actual culprit,' I said. He said, 'son, the legislation, things are more complicated than you know. If it were up to me I'd put all seven of them in jail, this is all I could do, I'm sorry,' he said. Still looking for the other five, right. Where would they be? They'll all be found in relatives' houses.

I haven't seen R. for three months. Yesterday I had my aunt call round her house. Her mother answered the phone, 'R. has gone to the village,' she said. So they've sent my R. to the village. My aunt is angry with me, why do you still want to talk to her, didn't she hand you over to her father and her brother... I'm not angry with her. I know her. I'm sure they forced her to call me. Who knows how they scared her, with what they scared her. Otherwise she wouldn't squeal on me. Not for the world.

I was going to enrol in a driving licence course next month, on the day I turned eighteen. And as soon as I got my licence I was going to go to Batman in my uncle's car and take R. on a spin. But I haven't been able to stick my nose out of the door ever since I came back home. How can I do my military service with this shame! How does one rape another man, you faggots! God damn you all!

My Sister

We strangled my sister; she haunts my dreams every night!

She went around with boys. She used to dress indecently. There was no end of the gossip in the neighbourhood. We warned her time and again... she wouldn't listen. Seeing there was no way out, the four of us men, along with my father, we sat down and talked. It is like this and this, we said. This girl is ruining our honour. She's wayward too.

We decided she should be quietly killed. We assigned İzzet, our youngest. One night we went into our sister's room while she was sleeping. İzzet wrapped the cable around her throat and tightened it. She didn't even find the time to fight back, she just opened her eyes wide and looked like she was sad for a few seconds, and then my sister was gone, just like that. We carried her body to the car. We took it to Şile and threw it into an empty field. Everyone in the family knew what we had done. We thought we had restored our honour. We thought we had done a clean job, but I can't stand it any more. My sister has been haunting me in my dreams every night for nine years! What we did was inhuman. Shame on us!

The Pillow Angel

As of tomorrow, unless the 'Ethics Committee' objects, I'm going to remain a child forever. Tomorrow, if my mother and father could persuade a few more doctors that they're doing this thing they're doing for my sake, they're all going to continue to mutilate me, all through my life.

They've been giving me hormones for three years so that I would not grow up any more. For I can't get off the pillow, I cannot walk or talk. They say it's the result of a rare brain disease. I'm nine years old. According to the Ethics Committee I have the intelligence of a three year old. The ignorance.

First, on cold operating tables, they stopped my breasts from growing. I got off that table with something missing each time I opened my eyes. Once I saw a scar on my stomach. Then there was one on my genitalia. I realized from what they said that they had first removed my appendix, then my womb.

Apparently they're doing this to improve my standard of living. Unless there's hormonal intervention, I could grow into a physically developed woman with a baby's intelligence, so they've been mutilating me with various hormones for three years. At the end of this hormone 'therapy' my height will be reduced by twenty per cent, and my weight by forty per cent. Apparently even this is not enough. Unless the Ethics Committee objects tomorrow, they're going to continue pumping hormones into my body. They are going to mutilate me non-stop. Mutilate non-stop.

Evolution / II

So you think you're so clever! As if!

An extensive survey of two hundred and fifty thousand people in Norway reveals that the eldest is the most intelligent one amongst brothers, and that is true also of boys who step up to the plate if the eldest dies. Who knew! The IQ differences among siblings are attributable, to the development of the children's status in the family hierarchy. Who'da thought it? Now I don't know whether the ape is the ancestor of the human beings, but if you were to understand a little bit better what that strange botanist calls 'Evolution' you would no longer be surprised that the 'middle' child is the one that strives most to assert himself. That the oldest child assumes the sexual, characteristic and even physical features of the stronger parent no matter what their own sex might be. That the younger child renders himself at least as weak as the weaker parent so that he would at least receive that parent's approval. That some siblings, on the other hand, leave their homes at dawn some day upon understanding that no matter what role or colour they assume they would not be able to find shelter in that house. What's so surprising about that? That's how we grow up at home, playing nice with our siblings, ever exiled from our selves. Pardon me?

I B-b-broke my Oath!

Now, dear m-m-mem-bers of the p-p-ress, I s-s-tand be-fore you like a fif-ty-one year old s-s-trange crea-ture that has just learnt to s-s-peak. I a-po-lo-gize for the s-s-slow-ness of my s-s-speech and for my voice being ve-ry low. As ma-ny of you know, my name is Rai-ner Her-pel*. I am an art-ist. I b-b-broke my oath. I dec-lare that to-day, af-ter the pass-ing a-way of my faa-ther yess-ter-day, I have put an end to my t-t-twenty-nine years of s-s-silence by s-s-starting to s-s-speak a-gain.

I have not said a word in t-t-twenty-nine years. The rea-son for that is my faa-ther and all the fa-scist pr-ac-tices that I p-p-pro-test in his p-p-per-son.

The on-ly thing I e-ver wan-ted to do in life was to p-p-paint. I was ac-cep-ted by the fine art s-s-school. Ev-ery-thing was go-ing won-der-ful-ly at s-s-school. I be-live-ed I was go-ing to be a good art-ist. My t-t-tu-tors were al-so of the same o-pinion. But my faa-ther ne-ver even blink-ed when he re-moved me from s-s-school, be-cause he wan-ted me to run the spa ho-tel we had in-herit-ed from my grand-fa-ther in our town, Bad Ems. He always ob-ject-ed to my be-com-ing an art-ist: He did-n't e-ven lis-ten to me.

For t-t-twenty -nine years I never s-s-said a word to any-one. I rare-ly went out of my room, I didn't ac-cept any vi-sit-ors. All I did was paint. My mother Walt-raut be-came my t-t-ton-gue. And when I did go out I shut my ears with ear-phones so that I w-w-wouldn't hear any noise. Many peo-ple re-acted qu-ite harsh-ly. They t-t-told me I was be-having child-ish-ly, that I was b-b-eeing a b-b-bur-den to my mother, that I was p-p-pun-ish-ing my-self rather than my faa-ther. But I had no words to say so long as I was sur-round-ed by a faa-ther who did not want to

---

* Rainer Herpel is a German painter who only resumed speaking again in 2002 after his father's death

hear me, and a fasc-ist world that drove one from one's own spirit. Honour-able m-m-mem-bers of the press, I am hoping that you will under-stand me; I, who have kept my s-s-self-res-pect only through remain-ing s-s-si-lent and have spent a whole life with various sac-rifices for my prin-ciples: Some-times one is left with no other way of shou-ting than remaining si-lent.

I'm Out of Sorts

Hello there uncle. What've you been doing? Give us a cup of tea, thank you. Eh, I couldn't sleep well last night man... I don't know. I'm out of sorts, for some reason... nah, it's not about my woman. Forget it uncle, don't start with marriage now. She's fine the way she is, let her stay that way. The kids? Well, I don't know really... they're growing up probably. I'm sure they're fine, their mother is sure to look after them. Uncle, what should the kids do with me, for God's sake, it'll all be fine, their mum will take care of them. Oh, I do send them stuff now and then. Thanks, thanks a lot, I've got money all right. They've named me Murat, haven't they: things come about when I want them to. Well, what can you do, you can't live a life without jokes, can you? It was funny though, wasn't it? Go on, laugh... that's it. My father? Why ever should I see that cuckold? What do you mean he's my elder, uncle, what father? Bloody bastard, forget it. He's ill? Hope he gets worse. Uncle, don't make me run on with my curses: Look, uncle, you'll get your share if you continue, eh... I swear I'll just take off, don't make me feel sorry I've come... first thing in the morning, for God's sake... I swear, don't make my blood boil. See you're still at it... get out of my way. I said get out. Let go of my arm man... I said let it go, I'm telling you, you're going to get hurt now... I swear I won't care that you're my uncle, I'll break your hand: Get out of my way uncle, let go of my arm! I said let go! I'm telling you, you're really making my blood boil! There, let go man... let it go, let it all go! Move aside! Good grief man! Why do you push me so uncle, I've told you a thousand times not to mention that man when I'm around: Why don't you just do as you're told: I swear, this is the last time uncle. I swear by my mother I won't ever see you if you mention him again. I swear to God: I've taken a great oath,

---

* Murat is a name meaning desire, wish, aim, and goal. (T.N.)

mind you. I swear... I swear to God. What was that? That's it... Now, that's good. Swear again, right, right, I've got it, fine. No need to hassle me like a woman. Give us another cup of tea then. Fine, I'm not leaving, go on with your work, I'll take a look at these newspapers here. Hey son, hand me that newspaper, will you... thanks. Now see that news... price increases, accidents, murder... man, isn't there a single bit of good news in this whole newspaper for God's sake. Good grief the world. Now see that, this was all the country needed, and it's happened! Did you read this? They say an Italian girl is missing... they say she was travelling from one city to another in a wedding dress. No uncle, she was making art or something... seems she's been missing for some days... How naïve you are, man, 'should anything ill have befallen her'... of course it would, what else? They probably raped her and murdered her. God knows what bastard did it. They're going to disgrace us in the eyes of the EU.

Baby Girl

I cried, I cried non-stop. I was only two days old and I could think of nothing but to cry. I said, girl, you just cry. Scream at the top of your voice. Why should God the Father, who gave you life only two days ago, grudge you a living! Let out a squeal. Make a fuss. That is how I kept myself going.

To be honest, I'm still surprised at all that has happened. I was sound asleep in my room at home; my mother had just nursed me. And how sweet sleep is for us babies!

Suddenly two arms, which I immediately knew were not my mother's by their smell, grabbed me out of my cradle. Before I could say 'Mummy, save me!' in the only language I knew he smothered my nose with something and I dropped off. Then, when I opened my eyes it was pitch black. It was dark everywhere. I let it rip.

I cried and cried but not a sound. I knew my mother was far away; otherwise she would have come running already. I realized that the situation was not good. Then I said, girl, why should God the Father, who gave you life only two days ago, take your life so soon? He's not a fool! He certainly made an effort in some way or other for you to be born. You just go on screaming.

I cried non-stop for two hours. Those doggies turned up just as I had given up hope. Then people came, you know the rest, I was rescued and I'm telling you my story.

When I grow up I'm going to feed doggies bones every day.

The Murderer of Celalettin

You don't know how powerful I am. How I work through disasters, to make them happen at the same time, and in similar ways. I love cycles.

I make sure the brains that are programmed to lose actually do lose, exactly the way they are programmed to, albeit unawares.

That guy Celalettin of Diyarbakir. You've probably read about it in the newspapers. He was in a traffic accident two years ago. His car was hurled into the opposite lane when its rear, right tyre had a blowout and he was run over by a speeding lorry. Celalettin's wife and his two daughters died there and then.

He didn't. He survived with injuries. After the accident he sank into a depression, naturally. Worse still, he was imprisoned for two months for having an LPG system illegally installed in his car, and for speeding.

But Celalettin of Diyarbakir was strong-willed. He wouldn't give in. He decided he would start a new family. He got engaged again, he even set the wedding date: third of February. What a man filled with the joy of life!

Today is 19 January; two years after the morning of the accident he steered into.

You don't know how powerful I am. In that dark place you simply call 'sub-conscious' and do not really take me seriously I am delicately preparing the new loss of Celalettin from Diyarbakir with my own hands. We'll see. He won't die unless he's destined to die tomorrow. I can't go that far. But he'll surely lose. He'll lose tomorrow, tomorrow next year, and tomorrow the year after that. Until a proper 'Expert' comes and stops me.

Evolution / I

Just a few days after I had greeted life, there was a slap on my face. Then another one. And another. And another. On my arms, on my legs: another one, and another one. Mother, mother, where are you? No sound. Another one. Just as I was saying, finally it stopped; let me catch my breath, another one. Mother, mother? She's not there.

Not there.

I opened my eyes in a cramped place. Things were connected to my nose, my chest, and my legs. I could not move. There was something on my bottom too, I had peed in it and not realized it. When?

There's a hand on my head. But it's not beating me, like my father did over and over again. It's stroking me gently. This hand caresses me. It's caressing me gently. Now that's good.

I'm very sleepy. I could sleep forever. At least there is no beating in this strange glass house of mine. A hand on my head; two holes made into this strange tiny house of mine – they call it an incubator – so that that hand could reach me. That hand is caressing me from there. I like that hand.

Later. Months later... apparently, I am an infant gorilla that was a victim of 'domestic violence,' an infant gorilla whose ancestors were driven from the forests of Africa into a zoo in the city of Münster, Germany. My neighbour told me months later, he had found out about my story from the newspapers. It appears that following my birth my mother abandoned me, for some reason. And my father, again for reasons unknown, started beating me, totally ignoring the fact that my eyes weren't even open yet. He beat me up day after day, one slap after another (did all that beating do you any good?). You see, while I was beaten up all the time all the time the zoo doctor saw me as he was wandered in our little forest we'd been allocated. He felt sorry for me. (Bless him), he saved me from my father's hands and brought me here. But I was in such a feeble, such a bad state that they first put me in this glass cage called an incubator to care for me.

The hand that caresses my head belongs to my doctor. I even have a name! Mary 2 (I wonder why 2?). As far as I've found out from my know-it-all neighbour the name is sacred for humans. As we are the closest to humankind, that name will be sacred for us too once our evolution is complete, appreciate your name, says my neighbour. Fine, I will. There's no harm in that. But I've decided that if I come across her, I'm going to ask my namesake very nicely: 'My Holy Namesake! Since you're holy, I would like to ask of you that from now on, no one should ever beat anyone. It's not a nice thing to do.' Yes, that is exactly what I'm going to say.

Petra

Like I don't know that that great big thing is plastic! They say I've been in love with the swan shaped plastic boat on which people go boating on Lake Aasee since the spring of 2006. They say I don't migrate with the other swans that fly south before winter arrives because I don't want to leave my beloved behind. They say that the authorities, who are upset that I'm in love with that plastic thing, are introducing me to bachelor males but I'm slighting them. They say this and they say that. They say that black swans fall in love only once in their life and that therefore it is highly likely that no one is going to be able to separate me from this black swan all of my life. So on and so forth. Am I an idiot? Of course I know that that huge thing is plastic!

Nevertheless, something I did one day out of fury suddenly became an inseparable part of my life. If that stinking Adler had not encouraged the hussy Gerda we would have had five or six kids already. I mean, he had the hots for me. I knew it. He answered my songs, we gazed at each other; our union could have taken place any moment. Yet Gerda had her eye on Adler all the time. Brazen hussy. I knew Adler is going to choose me but still but there was jealousy. When Gerda pushed her chest forward towards Adler that day I thought my man was going to respond to her; that he was going to go and touch her. I mean that is how close they were to each other: I went mad of course. Just wait till I avenge myself on that man, I said. Wait till I make him groan bitterly!

And it happened that right at that moment that huge thing passed by me with two giggling kids inside it! The idea struck me like a thunderbolt! It suddenly occurred to me, just like that. I tagged along behind it on purpose. So that Adler would turn green with envy. He did turn green, as a matter of fact, but other things happened as well! Some guy must have thought it was so funny that I was following this plastic (which indeed is a funny thing), that he took my photograph. My first photograph ever.

I'd be lying if I said I didn't like it. But darling, how could I have ever known that I would become so famous after that! That dozens of my photos would be taken! That I would be on television!

Adler begged and begged. He begged me until the last moment. Nearly missed the flock. Honestly, I can't say that it did not cross my mind for a moment. Never mind, Petra girl. What do you want to be famous for? You go on and migrate with Adler, start your family before you're over the hill. But alas, fame was too sweet. I did not migrate. Adler left with tears in his eyes; I, on the other hand, got used to being without him, a long time ago.

I'm going on a television show again this evening, I'm going to sing. Everybody is going to think I'm singing for that huge plastic thing of course but I'll actually be singing for Adler... I mean he deserves that much at least. Besides... perhaps he'll hear me and come back!

RETURN

Zobar and Başa

I spilt the beans to my Zobar this morning. He was over the moon! Crazy girl, he said. So you've known it all along, why have you been hiding it from me for days? I was scared, that's no lie, I was scared, I'd miscarried our first baby, see, so I was afraid I might not be able to hold onto this one too. He smiled at me, revealing his beautiful teeth and saying, you carry the whole world inside you, wouldn't you be able to hold a single tiny baby. For heaven's sake Başa Baby, let's go to a doctor right away, he said. We're gonna go to the Taksim Emergency tomorrow morning; I'll talk to my boss and take a day off.

My Zobar's been working for an electrician for eight months. How skilful he turned out to be too! Better than all the educated boys at the shop. His boss is very pleased as well. Eh Zobar, what a great man you'da made if you'd had an education, he said one day. Seeing my Zobar was upset he added immediately, but don't you worry, you'll still make a great man, I'll give you all the training you need, he said. My Zobar was so happy, just like a child.

We work near each other. Would'a been hard if we didn't anyway, says Zobar. He says we'll go to work together each morning and we'll come back together every evening. He says it would be impossible otherwise! We work near our home as well. His is in Galata, mine's in Tünel. I love my job. I'm responsible for all the books! The boss is amazed, 'how you managed to learn about so many books in such a short time,' she says. And I say, 'Madam Selmin, madam, a person can learn anything quite quickly if they really want to'. I'm allowed to read as much as I like when there are no customers in the shop. On one condition – that I have to be very careful. I'd never damage the books anyhow! You'd think I'd never touched them, I read so carefully.

Each morning, my dear Cingo and my little Tinke drop us off at work of course. Each parting is a misery! But we tell them, mummy and daddy are going to bring you nice food in the evening! Otherwise you'll have to roam the streets and find your own food like you had to once. Then they stop sulking and trot back to our neighbourhood because they love the bones we buy'em.

We're going to Edirne next month. No, we're not moving, we've found our place now, and we're not moving anywhere else, we're going to a wedding! The other day Coro and Mother Milay sent word: Yilo was getting married! Yilo, who'd given up when Leyla's father sent him packing! He had no daughter to give to a gypsy like Yilo. Still grieving for his brother Dobru, the lad literally gave up on the world. We all thought he would neither speak nor laugh again. Yet this is what I love about life: we human beings never tire of living.

The wedding's in June. We've already got our outfits: I found a backless red dress from Terkos Arcade. It's so beautiful! It's got roses on it. And a yellow suit for my Zobar! God, how handsome he is! Cingo and Tinke are gonna be out of sorts for a few days because we're leaving them behind but what can we do – no big doggies on buses. When we come back we'll kiss'em and cuddle'em till they have to stop sulking.

Lola'd not touched her pipe since the murder of her husband Dobru. Not a sound came out of her pipe, not even after all the insistence and her boss going all the way to Edirne to plead 'customers're asking for you, Nevizade street's no good without you, come back and I'll give you a raise'. She's finally gonna play at Yilo and Azime's wedding, I hear! I'll probably cry, don't think I can stop myself.

As for Sulukule: We don't go there any more. It hurts. They've pulled down almost all of the houses. Very few friends are left, and it's not certain whether they're going to stay any longer. People with money kept coming and taking people's houses from them. Brutes.

Our new neighbourhood is not that bad though! Although it's not like Sulukule in the summer evenings, sometimes we all get together downstairs and enjoy ourselves singing and dancing. There are some very nice people. There aren't so many Romani as in

Sulukule but still. Zobar and me, we get along well with everyone. Besides, we talk between us, we've seen it now, we've grown up enough to see it: where you live matters, sure, it matters all right, but people matter more. The other day I told Madam Selmin too, she really liked it. This is what I said: 'Madam, it does not matter so much which four walls you've made into your home or where. The only place a person will truly be comfortable in is the country they have inside... That's what I think!' She's a cold fish mind you, still she was moved by my words, she even had tears in her eyes! That means I said something right; you speak right, sez my Zobar when I told him about it in the evening. He gazed at me with those almond eyes of his and gave me a long loving tender kiss.

THE TRANSLATOR

AYŞEGÜL DENIZ TOROSER ATEŞ is a lecturer in the department of English Language and Literature at Istanbul University, Turkey. She is currently working on her PhD dissertation on the contemporary English novel. Translating literary and academic works into English and Turkish, Toroser Ateş translated *P Art and Culture* magazine into English throughout 2007 and 2008. Together with Nuri Ateş, she also translated Çiler İlhan's first short story book, *The Dream Merchants' Chamber*, as yet unpublished in English, which can be seen on Çiler İlhan's website www.cilerilhan.com.

THE AUTHOR

ÇILER İLHAN has worked as a writer (*Boğaziçi, TimeOut İstanbul, Trendsetter*), and an editor (*Chat, Travel & Leisure*) at different times during her career. In 1993, she was the recipient of the 'Notable Short Story Award' at the Yaşar NabI Youth Awards, and subsequently her stories were published in numerous literary magazines. Her essays, book reviews, travel writings and translations were published in magazines/newspaper supplements such as *Kitap-lık, Radikal Kitap, Radikal Cumartesi* and *TimeOut İstanbul*. She is currently the Editor-in-Chief of *Condé Nast Traveller Turkey*.

Çiler İlhan contributed to the anthology of stories entitled *Tales of the 1002nd Night* (Metis Publications, 2005) with her story, 'Vulgata'. *The Dream Merchants' Chamber* (Artemis Publications, April 2006) is the author's first book, which is composed of stories that allude to one another and carry traces of magic realism. İlhan's story, 'Zobar and Başa' was included in *TimeOut Istanbul Stories* (May 2007), and *Bozcaada Stories* (Yitik Ülke Publications, September 2009) included the story, 'Steppenwolf Meets His Mozart'. She contributed various essays to the 2010, 2011, 2012 and 2013 Festival Books of the İTEF İstanbul *Tanpınar Literature Festival* (Kalem Ajans). Her second story book, *Exile* (Everest Publications, March 2010), with its interconnected stories with themes ranging from the invasion of Iraq to women from Batman, and the fate of laboratory, received the *2011 European Union Prize for Literature* (www.euprizeliterature.eu) Ilhan then contributed with excerpts from different ITEF Festival Books to the *City-pick Istanbul – Perfect Gems of City Writing* (Oxygen Books 2013) Her story, 'Pippa', from *Exile* was included in the French collection *Écrivains de Turquie Sur les rives du soleil* (Galaade, 2013) along with 16 Turkish authors from Adalet Ağaoğlu, Leyla Erbil to Enis Batur and Mario Levi. Çiler İlhan is a member of Turkish PEN. (cilerilhan.com)

www.ingramcontent.com/pod-product-compliance
Lightning Source LLC
Chambersburg PA
CBHW051308250626
47155CB00009B/3481